DRIFTS

• • • • • • •

DRIFTS

KATE ZAMBRENO

RIVERHEAD BOOKS • NEW YORK • 2020

RIVERHEAD BOOKS
An imprint of Penguin Random House LLC
penguinrandomhouse.com

Image on page 60 (left): *Dog, Westtown, New York (Scruffy Dog), 1978* ©
1987, The Peter Hujar Archive LLC, courtesy Pace/MacGill Gallery, New York,
and Fraenkel Gallery, San Francisco; image on page 63 (right): *Patricia Cawlings,
Los Angeles, 1980* © The Estate of Sarah Charlesworth, courtesy Paula Cooper Gallery,
New York; image on page 110 © Agence photographique du musée Rodin,
Jérome Manoukian.

Library of Congress Cataloging-in-Publication Data
Names: Zambreno, Kate, author.
Title: Drifts / Kate Zambreno.
Description: New York : Riverhead Books, 2020.
Identifiers: LCCN 2019044797 (print) | LCCN 2019044798 (ebook) |
ISBN 9780593087213 (hardcover) | ISBN 9780593087220 (ebook)
Classification: LCC PS3626.A6276 D75 2020 (print) | LCC PS3626.A6276
(ebook) | DDC 813/.6—dc23
LC record available at https://lccn.loc.gov/2019044797
LC ebook record available at https://lccn.loc.gov/2019044798

Printed in the United States of America
1   3   5   7   9   10   8   6   4   2

BOOK DESIGN BY LUCIA BERNARD

For Sofia Samatar
Zero. Zero.

*It should be remembered that the bulk
of the work they were doing was preliminary:
sketches, notes, jottings.*

—CÉSAR AIRA, *AN EPISODE IN THE
LIFE OF A LANDSCAPE PAINTER*

. . . .

*a work that feels unfinished, thin, accounts
of indisposition and sickness, books to be
sick with, diaries, whispers and notes*

—FROM THE DELETED TWITTER
OF SOFIA SAMATAR

| SKETCHES OF ANIMALS
AND LANDSCAPES

In the summer of 1907, in a letter to his wife from Paris, the poet Rainer Maria Rilke meditates on three branches of heather placed in a blue velvet-lined pencil box before him on his desk. The splendor of these fragments, which had arrived folded into her previous letter, he has been admiring for days. The poet notes the various tones and textures of the heather, the radiant green flecked with gold like embroidery woven into a Persian rug with violet silk, the complicated autumnal scents within it, the depth, of the grave almost, and yet again wind, tar, turpentine, and Ceylon tea, but also resinous like incense. At this point, his marriage is almost entirely epistolary. His wife, Clara Westhoff, a sculptor, is back in their farmhouse in Germany, taking care of their young daughter, Ruth. She is no longer able to be the peripatetic artist, keeping her various studios in Paris and Rome, leaving Ruth with her grandparents in the country. Rilke writes to Clara that he is truly ashamed he was not happy when he could have walked in an abundance of this heather, when they lived together for that honeymoon year, noting the flowers of this urban summer— the dahlias and tall gladiolas and red geraniums. It is in these letters that he attempts a prose like the weather he details, language he will lift for his novel that will take him close to a decade to write. To see and to work, he writes to Clara. How different they are. It is in this letter, reflecting on the fragments of heather he had failed to observe when they were waving in fields before him, that Rilke delivers his insight into the impossibility of the day and its relationship to writing: "One lives so badly, because one always comes into the present unfinished, unable, distracted."

In the summer of 2015, I was supposed to be at work on *Drifts*, a book I had been under contract for almost as long as I had lived in this city, renting the first floor of a shabby Victorian house in a tree-lined neighborhood so remote it was almost a suburb. The title of the book came from a feeling, and I wanted to write through this feeling. What I really wanted to write was my present tense, which seemed impossible. How can a paragraph be a day, or a day a paragraph? But I couldn't often exist in the room, or even in this paragraph, now. I found myself always distracted.

The publishing people told me that I was writing a novel, but I was unsure. What I didn't tell them is that what I longed to write was a small book of wanderings, animals. A paper-thin object, a ghost. Filled with an incandescence toward the possibility of a book, as well as a paralysis. Maybe I was writing a novel, in the Robert Walser sense, his short forms like moods and digressions. "For me the sketches I produce now and then are shortish or longish chapters of a novel. The novel I am writing is always the same one, and it might be described as a variously sliced-up or torn-apart book of myself."

What is a drift? Perhaps a drift is a sort of form.

For some time, I have been interested in the writing one is doing when one is not writing. I email often throughout the day with Anna, a more successful writer, living in a different city. We have both been under contract for our respective novels for several years. Art is time, Anna writes me, a novel especially, it must be slow; it must take the time it needs. All that summer, I attempt time. I try not to let the days bleed. I attempt to be in the room, outside of the internet. That summer, along with my daily black journals that accumulate in rows like gravestones, I begin keeping a notebook that I think of as the *Drifts* notebook, its cover a canary yellow that matches my copy of Walser's *The Tanners*, which I read in short increments each season, never finishing.

I crane my head now and see the first of the yellow notebooks on the small table across the room, in a pile with other filled and partial journals, legal pads, printed-out notes, manuscript pages, photographs. Inside the yellow notebook I wrote my address and my name, except it was a slightly different version of my last name, which made me feel I had entered the space of fiction. The notebook was for a book called *Drifts*, but it is a different book from the one I'm trying to write now. I was surprised to find these notes inside the notebook. This *Drifts* desired to be a detective story, or maybe a murder mystery. Like something out of an Antonioni film. Searching for something lost or missing, but I didn't yet know who or what.

How summers are spent following my little black terrier, Genet, as he shifts into various dark shapes on the rug or wooden floor, following patterns of light. He paces nervously in the office, waiting at the door, eventually settling for a time on the fake-sheepskin rug under my desk, all these soft spots I plant for him around the house. He does not like to keep still within the office, it isn't close to any source of sunlight, to any window from which he can look out. To get any thinking done, I must ignore him, his desire to be fed, to play, his pushing the ball into my hand. I feed him my dried mango slices, which I eat so that I can chew on something leathery, chewing as thinking, thinking as chewing. In the morning, after John leaves for the museum, coffee after coffee, the key is not too many cups, and to remember to eat breakfast—granola, yogurt, and fruit, or toast after toast. The key is to remember to turn off the internet and to allow it to stay off. The key is to try to stay still. The distraction of Genet's bark. His periodic eruptions at possible intruders. His call-and-response to Fritz, the absurd blond Labradoodle next door who yelps from the window of the first floor of the pale yellow colonial. The psychotic burst of the mail slot, my dog's heart beating inside his small barrel chest. A low growl that builds as he flies through the house, careening around the corner, nails scratching, toward the front window, erupting at another delivery for the apartment upstairs, his sympathetic nervous system that I sponge from, his paranoia and intensity that I share. I see the postman smoking his brown little cigarettes outside the house. We wave at each other. I suspect he lights one after he visits here. He has seen me in various states of undress, after having been on the couch all day, staring at screens. How so often, when inside, I look at my inbox like an oracle, to remind myself that I still exist.

Fragile Fritz. Nietzsche's nickname. I tried to pet him once. He doesn't like other dogs or even other humans—a true loner. I also think of the Austrian writer Marianne Fritz, how she stayed inside with her scraps of paper, endlessly writing her dense and increasingly indecipherable body of work. I'm still obsessed with who is romanticized in literature as a hermit, and who, by staying inside, is viewed as simply crazy. The madness of writing versus the madness of not writing. Walser, who went to Waldau not to write, he said, but to be mad.

Throw away your notes, the unpublished male novelist advised me, in the depth of my spiritual crisis, the first summer here. This is when I was working on a different book, with the title of the name of a country. I wanted the book, like everything I have attempted these past years, to contemplate literary sadness. But all I had were my notes. Fragments of this book exist in open and wounded states, in notebooks, legal pads, boxes, endless notes, and files on my desktop. The male novelist sends me his notes on Nietzsche, written during his undergraduate years, with his anxious marginalia listing which philosophers remained unmarried. (Most, he observed, except Hegel.) Is it because of him that my fascination with the bachelor notetakers began? (Robert Walser, Kafka, Nietzsche, Wittgenstein, Joseph Cornell, Fernando Pessoa, and Rilke, too, pretended they were bachelors.) He was not yet thirty, frantic he'd not yet had a novel published. Like a twenty-eight-year-old Kafka, projecting himself, with ambivalence, as a forty-year-old bachelor in his diaries.

I am made of literature, Kafka confesses to Felice in an early courtship letter, recalling their conversation about Goethe when they first met, in the Brods' living room. I am nothing else and cannot be anything else.

All summer I sit in the broken Adirondack chair on the porch, existing in the present tense, in that trancelike state of seeing, like the animals. My notebook in my lap, my books scattered around me. The frequent desire to do nothing. How Genet stares at me, with his amber eyes, and I stare back. Somewhere in the piles on my desk, I could excavate a stained, partial printout of Susan Sontag's "The Aesthetics of Silence," which tells me that animals don't look but stare. I pull at my dog's little white Sontag mohawk as he rolls over for me to scratch his soft pink belly or I pick him up to kiss his little monkey muzzle. Genet is tranquil on the porch, sedated by the sun, as he gets up and collapses, alternating between patches of light, or shadow when his coat overheats. In summer we stare at the purple butterfly bush at the bottom of the steps, as the butterflies loiter about. But the landlord will cut it back in the fall, and last summer it didn't flower at all. A line from Sontag's journals I keep writing down in my notes: "All great art contains at its center contemplation, dynamic contemplation."

Quiet, quiet, I say to Genet as dogs walk by, which he obeys by ruffing softly yet firmly to himself. Together we watch the promenades of dogs in the neighborhood. I wave at the Nepalese woman who lives in the apartment building on the corner, walking the silver pit bull with sleek muscles who was a puppy when we moved here. There is the Yorkie who erupts constantly from her perch high up in a building in the middle of the block. How sensitive they really are, these city dogs, but they cannot see it in one another. The ice-eyed Alsatian puppy, gangly and manic, whose owner is an older, muscular trainer, always in shorts, who lives with his wheelchair-bound mother in one of the houses on the street. While writing this, I realize that the Alsatian is no longer a puppy now but a full-grown dog, yet retaining a puppy's jitteriness. I often wonder if the trainer thinks I'm lazy when he sees me on the porch in my sun hat, watching the procession of the neighborhood with my dog. But I am working, taking notes and thinking. Not just laziness, I've decided, but what Blanchot calls *désoeuvrement*, translated variously as "inoperativeness," "inertia," "idleness," "unworking," or my favorite, "worklessness." A spiritual stance, more active, like decreation. The state where the writing of the fragment replaces the work. Kafka filling up notebook after notebook at night, sitting in the living room, blanket on his lap, having to cover his cage of canaries until they quiet, everyone else in the family asleep. In his notebooks he complains about the factory, Felice, his family, and later about how much time the publishing of his first little book, *Meditation*, takes away from his potential literary powers. Although when finally confronted with publishing his writing, he is panicked with how little work has accrued from the hours he spends in the middle of the night on his series of notebooks, the fragments he has published occasionally in journals. The artifice, he complains to himself, of trying to prepare a text for publication, when what he desires is to let a work take shape unforced. What he desires is a new prose. I email Anna, asking whether I should rename my book *Meditation*, after Kafka, or *Contemplation*, an alternate translation. No!—a one-word reply. It is irritating, someone else's book crisis. The lists of titles she sends me as well. All this, of course, is fervent procrastination. That summer, we were both on a deadline—now your book is out, is on all the best-of lists. I am still here.

Only inside the house can there actually be solitude, writes Marguerite Duras. Outside the house, there is a garden; there can be cats and birds. "But inside the house, one is so alone that one can lose one's bearings." Only now, Duras writes, does she realize that she's been in the house where she's written her books for ten years. Only now do I realize I've been here for seven.

In *The Walk*, Walser's narrator takes leave of his writer's block, his room of phantoms, and goes on a picaresque walk around the town and countryside. How Walser in his shabby suit would walk for ninety miles, as a way to not exist, to disappear into the landscape. His walking, like his writing, a sign of his absorption. I want to write about the looping reoccurrence of the elderly woman on my walks with the dog. She must be in her nineties, living alone in the large, dilapidated yellow-and-brown house on the corner——the pale brown shingles on the roof splintering off. She wears a headband in her silver bob, somewhat girlishly, and a version of the same worn outfit around her skinny frame, usually a button-down blue or pink shirt with white stripes and a pair of men's beige trousers belted high. When the weather allows she is often perched near the pillar on her front porch stairs, opening her face to the sun. Sometimes she will be sitting with a little cat who's recently appeared, staring off into the distance. That is her outside cat, she tells me, she also has an inside cat. I wave at her, and sometimes she waves back. I will see her then taking in the chair. Sometimes for long stretches of time there will not be a chair outside and I will worry about the woman. I think of her often, in that large gaping house alone. Perhaps she goes somewhere, where there's better weather. Maybe she has family somewhere.

There are seasons when I see the old woman regularly, usually on morning walks to the train station to see John off to work. Other times, I will go a month without spying her. When we pass and exchange hellos, she repeats one of a few phrases: Nice day for a walk, or Nice doggy. Sometimes I see her away from her porch and her garden, moving slowly down the street. There is something of my mother in this woman, if my mother had ever been allowed to grow old. Perhaps it's that my mother was often found crouched in our suburban front yard, in her khakis, pulling weeds. When I do speak to the old woman, she comes closer to me, as I suspect she cannot hear much of anything—which might also be the reason for her canned phrases—and reveals a mouth of gold and rotten teeth. A nice day for gardening, I say, and she follows her script: People think I'm poor, she says, because I don't hire anyone, but my doctor says it's good exercise. Your shrubs look elegant this year, I tell her, although the grass is becoming brown and dry, which I do not mention. Often she asks me what day it is, and sometimes I tell her, but in the summer, when all the days begin to bleed together, I sometimes will not remember, and we stand there, for a moment, having no idea where we are in the week.

Who are the characters in your novel, the publishing people ask me, and does anything happen?

In a book about architecture, I read that the space of the neighborhood is the space of childhood. And I feel like I'm in my childhood again, walking and biking around the tree-lined neighborhood, empty like a ghost town in the summer. Last summer, on a morning walk, I spied one of the little dogs I remembered from a missing-dog flyer, fresh ones continually replacing torn and faded ones, as he disappeared behind one of the vacant and run-down Victorian houses that look ruined in the light. For weeks afterward I biked around looking for the little white ghost Chihuahua, who had been so alarmed when we came near it, mostly because Genet had decided to freak out as well. I worried over it, scared and trembling, on its own.

I felt spooked by the gaze of the feral cats when we first moved here, as I came upon them in alleys and drive-ways, in pairs and threes, like silhouettes or ghosts, star-ing at me, skirting back if I got too close while trying to take their photograph. An old man used to feed a large colony that gathered outside of his house on 19th Street, until he died and the house stood abandoned. Eventually the son came in and repainted the house and put it up for sale. Now it's one of the new and renovated mansions, amidst so many others that remain run-down and empty. Its grand porch is vacant now, absent of the crowded postures of the unblinking cats. Where did they go?

Since moving here I have been obsessed with a tiny striped cat, an orphan who disappears for months at a time. I call her the raccoon cat, because of her patterned tail and striped coat. The previous winter I was convinced I could hear her from outside my bedroom window, an eerie cry like a changeling's, and the next morning I'd put on my boots and trudge around in the snow, attempting to find her. Later that spring I saw her perched, as if surprised, on top of a trash can in the alley, gnawing at the remnants of a slice of pizza. I began to lure the cat to my stoop with sardines and cat food, despite my dog's protests. She would frequently dart away if I came too close. Sometimes, though, she would let me sit on the chair while she ate underneath the bench, and I would feel such joy, watching her little tongue go in and out. Other times I was content to watch her eat from the window. Soon other strays began to frequent the porch, and I would feed them as well, although I was less attached to them. I marked in my notebook whenever I saw the cat, keeping track of her comings and goings. In this way, as with keeping track of my interactions with the old woman, I felt that I was at work on my novel. But the cat will disappear for months, worrying me, until I see her dart beneath a parked car, raccoon tail waving. I still refuse to name her.

When I first moved here, I taught a graduate writing seminar on the fragment at one of the liberal arts colleges. In each of the three fragmentary novels we read, a different narrator, experiencing a declining mental state, exacerbated by loneliness, worried over her lost cat. In each of the three, it's unclear to the reader whether the cat actually exists. I said to my students then, over the uncanniness of this repetitive narrative thread across several books: Perhaps this is true loneliness. You worry over a lost cat you don't even know exists. Everyone wrote in their notebooks when I said this, as if I had said something profound.

Suzanne and I are always trying to reach each other, sending little missives, trying to set up chats. It used to be easy, when we had each other's blogs to read, that showed what it felt like to be inside our days. Still it's when we read each other's work that we feel the closest. I write to her of my feelings of isolation, being off social media. I began to find it hard to be alone, when I used to love my solitude, I write to her. I scattered myself in fragments online. But still I google myself constantly. It's a sickness. Suzanne is now reading May Sarton's *Journal of a Solitude*, at my urging. She has just moved into her own apartment, separated from her poet husband, who is now dating a woman—worse, another writer—worse, a poet with a PhD and tenure-track appointment. Suzanne has been torturing herself online looking at pictures of them at literary functions together. How this taps into her isolation already, the community she has lost with the separation. Everyone says it's so healthy to have friends, she writes to me, but I find it sometimes more isolating. The self-harm of social media—we both understand it and yet feel compelled by it, these pictures and narratives of success and happiness, however fictional.

I last saw Suzanne that May, when she stayed with us for an event for her book. There were only a handful of people in attendance—a couple of people she knew, my editor, two of my students, an ardent bookstore employee. I was supposed to bring in the audience, I think. That summer, we communicate infrequently, but when we do, she talks about her ex, his new life. She must derive some pleasure from this rage, she writes me, otherwise why can't she let it all go, her past life? For years she will cycle through this rage and despair, the grief of her divorce, fragments I let her repeat because I know she needs to. But Elena Ferrante is not a School of Emotional Coping! I try joking to her that summer. How exhausted I am after she stays here, having to be so emotionally available, although I also long to spend time with her. It's uncomfortable sometimes to be in such close proximity with another woman. I see it in the ways we withdraw, have to repair inside. That's what writing is for us. That interior space.

One day, while taking the dog out for a walk, I come upon two Post-it notes on the sidewalk outside of the house. It takes a while for me to realize they are marked with my handwriting. I must have thrown them out, and my notes scattered into the street. I have saved them, crumpled, on my desk somewhere:

> *Urgent need to communicate*
> *Urgent need to disappear (withdraw)*

The last notes Kafka ever wrote, when he was in the sanatorium, dying of consumption, slips of conversation to his nurses. Writing as X-ray. His last note was something like, To think I could simply venture a large swallow of water.

That summer, I begin to bleed so heavily and for such an extended period of time that I feel sure I am entering peri-menopause, even though I am only thirty-seven at the time. I can't find any system to reliably contain it. One day, escaping to a restaurant to write in my notebook despite the heat, I stain the wooden patio chair with my blood. I try my best to clean it up, spilling water over it, mopping it up with paper napkins, my fingers smudged with blood. Finally I slink out of the restaurant, avoiding all eye contact from the smoothly sincere waiters, and creep home, weeping. I don't go back there for months. On the toilet I bleed out large clumps of a fascinating and wobbly texture, examining the clumps with my fingers, while calling and texting everyone I know with a middle-aged uterus. My ob-gyn sends me to get vaginally probed to assess the size of a new cyst growing on my ovary. She puts me back on birth control, which makes me so psychotic that one day I make turkey sandwich after turkey sandwich, like an assembly line, eating each one until I make myself sick.

I am supposed to travel for an event, but I cancel it. I cancel almost everything.

Our housekeeper, who comes twice a month, a Peruvian grandmother named Beatriz, shows me her surgery scars, pulling her sweatpants down to one side. She had her ovaries removed at home near Lima, she tells me, it was cheaper there. In response I pull up my shirt and show her the scars on my abdomen. I often feel lazy, and rather wretched, having someone else clean the house while I'm at home, sometimes having abandoned work and watching something on my computer with headphones, finding it difficult to think or work with someone else in the house with me, making various sounds. She has cleaned the house for years, well before we moved in. But I also like having her here. I appreciate the company, someone to drink coffee with. I follow her around, helping her move furniture. She reminds me of my grandmother's family, many of whom cleaned house as well, including for my grandmother, when she got too old.

How strange not to be fertile anymore. A large part of me would feel relieved, that this was decided for me, in a way. I look at babies and know I'm supposed to want one. But John is mostly against it—overpopulation, climate change, money, our art, our lives, maybe we'd travel again—and I wasn't for it enough to argue against him or even myself persuasively. Maybe when we're older, we tell each other, and we're making the work we want to. And yet we are already older. I have given up so much, at this point—abandoning trying to get into a PhD program to be in the running for a full-time job, giving up having a baby. All I had left was the precarious life of a writer.

Although I am not sure I ever really believed I was fertile. It seemed odd to have never gotten pregnant, after two decades of being convinced in the dark, when I was tired, please, it just felt so much better without condoms. A poet and translator I once knew told me that when they looked at their breasts in the shower they thought, It's impossible that milk could come out of them, it's physically impossible. I suppose in a way that's what I always felt about myself. And that perversely my body would obey those feelings. And yet my body constantly betrayed how I wanted it to act or be.

I never understood why David Markson has his Kate bleed constantly in *Wittgenstein's Mistress*. Are we supposed to think she's going through menopause, as if the aging female body is always speculative fiction? Maybe that's what he thought a middle-aged woman's body would be like when entirely alone—naked, without maxi pads, bleeding clumps into the sea.

I was finally coming to terms, living here, with becoming a hag, which was becoming invisible. My striped hippie poncho and hairy legs and big straw hat in the summertime. Perhaps being a hag was like being a hermit—there was a grace and severity to this vocation.

I realize, writing this, that I have not had my period in some time. I don't have that to mark time anymore, the obliteration of the pain, the days elapsed in bed.

For the rest of the summer I begin trying to live a regimented day, an almost ascetic life. To avoid stress, inflammation—in the body and the mind. How ritual-istic, almost superstitious, I try to become—two hours in the morning of no email, no self-googling, exercise, prepare lunch, two more hours in the afternoon. Try to practice the Ayurvedic rituals I tape to my bathroom mir-ror. I like having my days structured for me. Blink my eyes seven times upon waking. Scrape my tongue seven times. Neti pot. I hold coconut oil in my mouth, which tastes like semen, then spit it out in the trash so as not to clog the pipes. Dry-brushing. Oil massage. Quick shower. Water with lemon before coffee. Yoga at noon. Or bike to the local college to swim. Grocery store. Then I make myself lunch—poached salmon, red quinoa, something green. My hands cold from washing kale for dinner. Return to work, if I am able. It's exhausting, trying to think and work with all this housework. In the afternoon, I often let myself sink into the couch and the internet. Anyway, I be-come run-down if I'm too productive, if I push myself too much. I begin going to community acupuncture weekly, lying back on a lawn chair in the middle of the yoga studio, trying to shut out other whispered sensitivities, a line of needles on my abdomen, a heat lamp suspended above.

Kafka's naked calisthenics in front of the open window, even in the winter. In an August diary entry, Kafka writes that even though he has failed to write a word that summer, he has gone swimming almost every day at the Civilian Swimming School in Prague. He finally has conquered, he writes, some of the despair over his body, his frailty.

Isn't it hard though, Anna writes, to be so healthy and in your body while being in your mind and your private world? The world of the body and sharing that, and the world of the work, the retreat?

Lately I have been thinking about Rilke for a story I'm
hoping to write. His inability to work in the summers,
this pattern that forms in the letters: escaping the urban
summer, the country versus the city. In letters Rilke
writes to Lou Andreas-Salomé from a red garden cottage
in the Roman suburbs, where he's followed Clara, who
has her own separate studio there. Rilke complains about
the humidity, the lifeless museum atmosphere, the ghast-
ly hordes of German tourists. Their finances a constant
worry. So much of his correspondence spent negotiating
publishing contracts, payments, trying to secure future
commissions. He must earn a living by writing. The
next place he lives must be decided by the work he is
doing, he writes. It is here that he begins to conceive of
the novel that would take him six more years to finish—
thinking through his hysterical Danish nobleman, going back to his initial, bewildering solitude in Paris.
He asks for his letters to be returned. He plans mono-
graphs he'll never write: one, on a poet, will necessitate
a trip to Copenhagen, another, on a painter, requires a
trip to Spain. He must learn Danish, continue Russian,
and translate more from the French. He complains of
his claustrophobia, nerves, toothaches. Later, in Berlin,
where Clara has taken another studio, he suffers an

impacted tooth, swollen gums and face. All the inter-
ruptions the day brings, the worries about money, the
smells. Everything that infects his transcendence. He
begins looking for a remote place with a good winter. A
refuge in Capri. It is difficult tracing his peripatetic life,
even then—is he fleeing the last room or going toward
the next? In Rome, he longs to get a dog, for companionship, but he doesn't let himself. What if he wants to
travel? He is no longer working on the novel.

Rilke had met Lou Andreas-Salomé when he was
twenty-six and she was a decade older. She was married
to a famous older scholar, but the marriage was uncon-
summated. The young René Maria had no back to his
head, she wrote in her diary: all the wisdom just fell right
out. She renamed him, giving him a proper German first
name under which he would be published. She tutored
him to change his handwriting to a smaller, more exacting
script, and disciplined him to make his prose less florid.
She had sent him alone to Florence, instructing the
novitiate to keep a journal of the art he saw there. Some
speculate this was her way to find space to think and
write, away from her devouring, much younger lover,
prone to violent moods and tantrums. One biographer
speculates that, at the age of thirty-eight, she sent him
away so that she could have an abortion.

Up at night arguing with John. Our shared misery. His constant desire to move out of this city, so that we don't spend everything on rent, so that he can have a studio. It also doesn't seem like you are happy here, he says. I'm not sure sometimes whether happiness is possible. Stuck on the couch, on days I can't manage to structure. It's the summers that are so paralyzing. I complain to John all day over chat while he's at the library. How empty it feels in this city. How far it feels to reach the other. We are looking for new spaces, but what we are really looking for is retreat, clarity, to escape our internal chaos. For the days not to feel glued together.

In her journal May Sarton asks, Can art be happy, does it have to be depressed? Her meditation on the small pink roses at her desk. Like Rilke's twigs of heather. It is only when she is alone, she writes, that she can see the flowers, that she can really pay attention to them.

It seems impossible, Anna writes me, to work on a novel while living with another person. It seems contrary to what is necessary to write a novel, which is to be alone.

And when her boyfriend is home her space becomes domestic, she becomes domestic. . . .

There's a line from the opening crisis of *The Notebooks of Malte Laurids Brigge*: "My God, if any of it could be shared! But what would it *be* then, what would it be? No, it is only at the price of solitude."

Need to figure out—what does Rilke mean by "it."

"*Today* is a word only suicides ought to be allowed to use; it has no meaning for other people"—the opening page of Ingeborg Bachmann's *Malina*, the truest line about writing a novel ever written. Every morning the unnamed narrator walks to her café to read the newspapers. Her lover nearby, her partner at home, in the Vienna neighborhood where she's lived for years. As company, she has a secretary to whom she dictates her correspondence. Dreaming, nightmaring, remembering, swooning, despairing, putting on lipstick, looking at wrinkles in the mirror, making notes of book titles, buying a new dress, reading philosophy, talking on the phone, drinking coffee, smoking, going to conferences, replying to letters . . . but never any writing.

The narrator in *Malina* wants to write a happy book for her boyfriend, Ivan, who also wants her to be happy, not in despair. This is probably why she's blocked.

The desire, in yoga, for my mind to be still—to be able to meditate on nothingness, to penetrate the day, to reset. Yet throughout class I make notes in my head for the book. "Monkey brain," my favorite teacher calls it. I escape to the toilet to scribble down notes on my phone. Thoughts about what it's like to be in the day and my body. That I should write about Kafka's digestion. The disgust he felt at his body. The attempt to relieve his constipation—a rhythm in the diaries. The lists he makes of his meals, his high-fiber vegetarian diet. His father's irritation at his son's breakfast, his yogurt, chestnuts, dates, figs, grapes, almonds, raisins, berries, whole grain bread, oranges.

There is a tremulous grace to how Genet squats, his back curving, as I stand over protectively, sometimes impatiently, for he can be very particular about where he chooses to go, and will take his time sniffing and nosing in the grass, sometimes pausing to sniff another dog's poop, and then the quick shuffle he performs afterward, kicking up grass, though I admonish him not to. In the heat my dog's shits are softer and more pungent, I must scrape the plastic bag through the grass.

All that summer, handwritten signs are posted on nearby trees, signs that become progressively angrier, asking people to pick up their dogs' shit, large scrawled black magic marker letters riddled with misspellings and colloquialisms. "Don't be a McNasty!" When the rains come, the signs stay up, becoming blurry and illegible, the marker bleeding across the paper underneath the clear packing tape, until they are finally taken down.

I masturbate throughout the day, so much that I pull a muscle in my writing hand, which makes me feel like Robert Walser. The herbs I've started taking to try to shrink the cyst make me unbelievably horny. I know, I masturbated five times this morning, Anna writes me. The summer recreation of the middle-aged woman novelist. I jump on John when he gets home from work, even though Genet protests with yelps when we are affectionate. Perhaps I think this will take the edge off my loneliness, which is severe in the summer. Or maybe my loneliness somehow is what makes me horny.

My editor later reads this above passage, and wants to inquire exactly why the narrator is masturbating. Is it to relieve excess creative energy, or because she has the time, or . . . ? I don't really know what to say. She masturbates because she masturbates.

No to everything, to all events, to all commissions, to requests, to living online, which leaves us with our novels. But when we look at what we've written, we hate it. Anna just looked at her notes for her novel and wants to throw up, she writes me. I think you have PMS, I write to her. I know, my cycle comes a week later.

Anna seems always to be traveling for weddings. We never go to weddings, and I feel smug about this. I don't know anyone who would invite us to a wedding!

I think about how John and I became artists to try to live a life of the mind, of active contemplation. My desire to write a novel that contains the energy of thought. Is this why I felt such crisis moving here? That was not the conversation.

The ants swarm on the porch—how fast and slow at the same time.

The irritation, I write to Anna, of being asked only to do events with women writers, or about feminism. The irritation of appearing only on these lists of women writers. The irritation of being referenced only in the context of other women writers, including each other. The irritation of being expected to read only other women writers, or to be read as a woman writer. Dreading the conversation our next books will inevitably be forced into. Dreading the comparisons. I want this next book to be completely new, as if from a completely different writer, I write to her.

I write to Anna, *Drifts* is my fantasy of a memoir about nothing. I desire to be drained of the personal. To not give myself away.

I think about May Sarton writing in *Journal of a Solitude* about becoming depressed upon every trip to New York, every entrance into publishing culture. How eager she is to return alone to her New England farmhouse. What a balm that book was for me when I first moved here. That the real work is one of solitude. How seriously Sarton takes her moods, her wrestling in the dark. Her fears, her rages, her depressions. The paralysis of bad reviews. "My need to be alone is balanced against my fear of what will happen when suddenly I enter the huge empty silence if I cannot find support there."

So often now I just want to weep—what am I mourning?

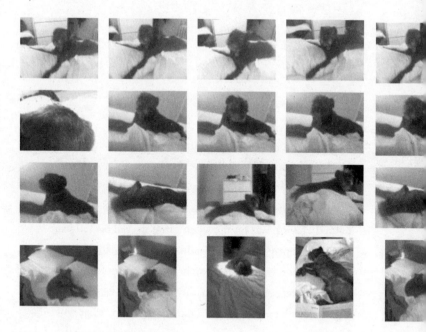

In my photographs, my dog's body becomes a landscape. I see him getting grayer with the years, scruffier and heavier in the winter. His grizzly face with his scraggly gray beard. As I write this, I look at him—we've just been in from a long walk in the snow, his paws in slushy puddles, and his hair is matted. When is the last time he's had a bath?

When it is too hot to be outside, I take pictures of him as we roll around on the white bed. His black fur makes him a difficult subject. He curls around the glowing af-

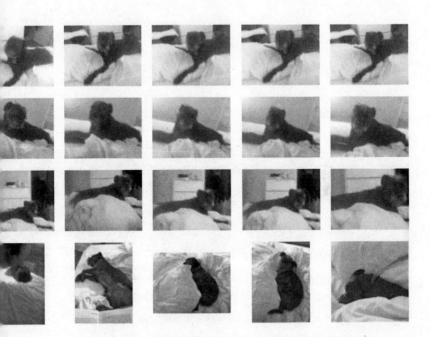

ternoon light coming in through the back window. We
stare at each other. When I masturbate, folded over the
bed on my stomach, he becomes concerned, begins to
hump my leg, then lies next to me and stares stoically in
the distance, as if he is protecting my space and privacy.
The pile of wilted black clothes on my dresser that I never
put away.

I am reminded of May Sarton feeding the outdoor cats
but looking for animals to hug at night. How hard I have
hugged Genet lately. My mind spinning and stupid.

"What prevents a book from being written becomes the book itself"—found in my notebook, citing the notebooks of Camus, who was himself quoting Marcus Aurelius.

What prevents me from writing the book? The heat, the dog, the day, air-conditioning, desiring to exist in the present tense, constant thinking, sickness, fucking, groceries, cooking, yoga, loneliness and sadness, the internet, political depression, my period, obsession with skin care, late capitalism, binge-watching television on my computer, competition and jealousy over the attention of other writers, confusion over the novel, circling around but not finishing anything, reading, researching, masturbating, time passing.

A fluorescent green Post-it note is on my laptop when I return from a walk: "How to fold time into a book?"

Constant real estate listings—another sickness that Anna and I share in these months, although we live in different cities. We look online for cabins or crumbly houses in rural areas. Anything to escape the heat and toxicity of the city. Anything to avoid working on our books. John is at war again with our landlord. Escalating rents we cannot afford. John insists we need to leave. He desperately wants his own studio. We constantly bicker over this. I need to stay, for the novel. Over the years, faint cracks have been spreading slowly across the walls. There are cracks at the corners of the moldings of the windows and the doors. There is a problem with the foundation. Yet we are still here.

The newlyweds live for a year in a solitary house on the moors, the wind circling the walls. It was a house they built so that they could work, a utopian project soon abandoned (a failure of Rilke's theory of an ideal marriage as each partner appointing the other to be a guardian of their solitude). Rilke is at work on one of his first experiments with prose. He has occupied a bedroom for his office. Clara's busts are scattered throughout the hallways, overflowing from her studio. On his desk of heavy mahogany a set of candlesticks, small notebooks. He can look out his window at the flowers, the fruit tree, the vegetable garden. His little black dog at his feet. Their daughter, Ruth, was born that December. The snowed-in cabin. The walls closing in. The crying baby. On a single day in January, when his daughter is five weeks old, he writes fourteen letters. Finally he receives a commission to write a monograph on the famous sculptor Auguste Rodin in Paris with whom Clara apprenticed. He had wanted his family to give him some solidity of self, mooring him to one place. He had longed for a monastic life. And yet he always needed to escape.

At the end of August 1902, the poet arrives in Paris
and takes a room at a run-down boardinghouse on
the Left Bank, the same address he will give to his alter ego, in the partially autobiographical novel he will
begin working on, or intend to work on, for almost a
decade, a novel he originally titles *The Journal of My
Other Self*. One year later, he writes of the oppressive
heat of late summer as a time when one goes through
smells as through many sad rooms, like the iodoform,
pommes frites, and fear coming through his character's
window. In this same letter, he rehearses the opening
of his novel, wandering through a series of interior and
exterior spaces, the hotel room, the library, and especially the hospitals. How fascinated and repulsed Rilke
was by the massive Hôtel-Dieu, the city's oldest public
hospital, by the long building with its gates wide open,
this gesture of impatient and greedy compassion. When
he passes the Hôtel-Dieu for the first time, an open
carriage is just pulling in, from which a person hangs
like a broken marionette, an oozing sore on his long, gray,
dangling neck. He writes to Clara, You can see all the
sick people in their sad, pale uniforms of illness, standing in the windows there. These masses haunt Rilke,
the factory-like production of anonymous deaths add
to his lifelong horror of sickrooms. He has his Danish
nobleman go for shock treatments at La Salpêtrière,
walking through the courtyard where people wearing white caps, which make them look like convicts,
stand among the bare trees. The endless rows of people
crowded shoulder to shoulder in the waiting room, all

from the lower classes, he notes, the air stale with soiled clothing and breath. A contrast to the photographs that Eugène Atget took in 1909 of the empty outdoor spaces of the courtyard and front facade of Charcot's famous hospital, where he treated late-nineteenth-century hysterics. Atget photographed his exterior spaces of Paris at dawn, because his old-fashioned equipment required a longer exposure time, giving the effect of a city emptied of its inhabitants.

In the apartment complex across the way there's an assisted-living facility. When it's hot, people in wheelchairs and their aides sit outside, sometimes smoking, seldom speaking. Sometimes the nonambulatory residents are wheeled outside on stretchers. Every Thursday and Friday I see the people come by with carts carrying large trash bags of cans, collecting them in the alleyway. The Japanese mother and daughter in the apartment building directly across from us who often ride by on a tandem bicycle. Sometimes the mother is dressed like she is going to a nineties rave, and other times she looks like she stepped out of the nineteenth century. There is the old hunched-over man, who wears socks with sandals, who carries a black plastic bag that I believe contains his other shoes, who sometimes sits on the tree trunk to the right of us, in front of the alley of the massive apartment building always littered with trash. He sits on the stoop and sometimes reads circulars of coupons he found on the street. Sometimes he leaves his bag of shoes there. He does this all so slowly.

When we moved here I would make lists of all the trash that surrounded the sidewalk near the alley, and the trash that blew into the yards of the large Victorian houses. How Genet would trot out to the same little bare patch of grass on the sidewalk, and with legs trembling pee over the mini Smirnoff bottle that must have been there for a year. How he would pee for a time over the same image of a naked woman from a faded magazine, or the pale blue tampon applicator. The garden has now grown, wild and green, no distinction between weeds and flowers. Sometimes I would write down lists of the trash scattered about: pink smashed Starburst candy, ketchup packets, Day-Glo straws, empty box of granola bars, tiny empty bottles of cheap hard alcohol, chicken bones, dirty diaper, dog shit. In the winter the way the trash and the cigarettes froze inside the blocks of ice, the dog shit remaining petrified and white after the thaw. I wonder if, by making lists of these ugly things, I was trying to make them somehow beautiful.

That summer, I meet Anna for dinner in the city while she is briefly in town. It's unusual, as I almost never leave my neighborhood in the summer. It was the second time we had met in person. I look so much more New York than the last time, Anna says to me, as if critically. I had more New York shoes, it was true. How uncomfortable writers can get when they don't live here, when they come to New York briefly, that crisis over what they are wearing. I felt it for the first two years I lived here, the panic of my body in public. Then I began to develop a uniform, a sort of armor. To meet Anna, I wore a white tank top and a slinky black jersey skirt and heeled sandals. How carefully I dress for other women. At dinner, Anna wants to talk about what I thought Elena Ferrante looked like. Surely she has the face of a novelist, the real face of a writer, Anna says. I had an interesting face too, she says, looking at me critically again. I don't know what that means. I don't know how having a face has anything to do with being a writer.

Can you believe that we met at that cheesy photoshoot? Like Sylvia Plath in *Seventeen*, Anna writes me after we see each other. It was the first time I had been photographed for anything. Anna had borrowed the shirt I brought with me, as we were supposed to bring something black to wear. She still uses the image as one of her author photos—staring intently, such clarity in her gaze, wearing my shirt, which Anna always notes was too big on her and had to be pinned in back. For my photograph, they chose one with my eyes closed, because otherwise, they said, I looked too intense. How ashamed I felt—about all of it. That I looked so passive with my eyes closed, like it was a death mask rendered in black and white. That I had agreed to participate at all.

After our dinner, I began to wonder whether Anna really felt close to me, or whether she keeps me close to make sure my work wasn't going to surpass her own.

In June, while sitting outside on the porch, I noticed
that a baby cardinal fell into our garden, because of the
squawking of its father nearby. (The internet tells me
that, among cardinals, fathers are the dominant parents.) I placed the baby bird on a higher branch, and
Genet and I monitored the situation all day, from the
window. At some point I looked and it was gone. I told
myself it had been rescued or had figured out how to
fly, but I knew most likely it was eaten by one of the
neighborhood cats, maybe even my cat. In yoga class,
led by the teacher who always asks us to share too much,
we are supposed to go around the room and say what
"father" means to us, as it was just after Father's Day.
Usually I pass, but that day I share the story about the
cardinal. The teacher replies that a psychic recently told
her that her deceased father's spirit animal was a cardinal. When she says this, she looks into my eyes and I
see that she is tearing up. I know I am supposed to feel
a meaningful connection, and I smile back, holding her
gaze, but inside I squirm.

Afterward, I think of the story of Wittgenstein at his
hermitage in Ireland. Apparently, he fed the seabirds
on his windowsill, eventually feeding them out of his

hands. Like something out of a fable about St. Francis of
Assisi. Wittgenstein even splinted an injured bird's wing
that fell into his garden. Once he left, the cats came by
and ate the birds, for they had grown too domesticated.
He was there at the cottage on the sea working on
Philosophical Investigations, a text he wrote while rest-
lessly wandering to various coastal and mountain landscapes, attempting a more monastic life. He writes to
a friend that prior to coming to Ireland he felt so ill and
depressed—a constant refrain for Wittgenstein—that
he hadn't gotten any writing done for six weeks. While
working on these notes, I keep on rereading the introduction to *Philosophical Investigations*, where he writes,
"The philosophical remarks in this book are, as it were,
a number of sketches of landscapes which were made in
the course of these long and meandering journeys."

"It's mystical, my relationship to language. When I sit down to write I never know where I'm going." George is in town to read from his new novel, a haunting work of prose from the point of view of a young woman, published on a small yet prestigious experimental press. The few reviews he receives compare him to Beckett, Calvino, Cortázar, and so on. The reading was an intimate gathering, which I always feel guilty about, as if I am expected to know people to bring to events in New York. We are talking at the bar across the street from the bookstore after the event. How I can cringe at language like this that feels received. At what point does the writing teacher begin to sound like a guru? At what point did we all begin to sound like writing teachers? Language is rife with contradictions, I say. I don't think it's mystical. It's that knowing is impossible. I want to get to a space without words, I said to George, but what then? To get to a space without words, are you then cured of writing? Like Wittgenstein attempting to overcome philosophy. I am skeptical of the writer who thinks of language as sacred. But there must be some joy in this act of writing. That longing of Kafka's for the force of his language to finally take place unshaped. That ecstatic feeling, once he wrote "The Judgment" in one sitting, from ten o'clock at night till six o'clock the next morning. Finally he had conquered time, staying up all night writing. His legs so stiff he couldn't pull them out from the desk when he was finished. The fearful strain and joy he experienced then.

The hushed and mournful tones speaking of a male novelist who had died, whom I had never cared to read. Everyone is solemn, but I wonder whether any of them had read him, or just thought they were expected to mourn. None of them actually knew him in person. I wanted to joke to the group, But isn't the author already dead?

Last summer a television set was dumped in the center of the sidewalk, and the sanitation workers refused to take it. Every day I would stop over it and stare into its broken face. There have been several television sets abandoned in the alley since then. I exchange the occasional email with a young writer in Idaho, another of my correspondents I have never met in person, about what we've been watching on TV. The previous spring I had emailed him to ask whether I should binge-watch *Taxi*. He thought it was a good idea. There is something so deeply comforting, he wrote to me, about a formulaic series—you can almost remove yourself as a viewer and don't have to be an active participant. The craving for a new show to binge, how it can be a way to structure the day, or become lost in it. I watched a couple episodes of *Taxi* and realized what I really wanted to do was watch the opening credits—Tony Danza driving over the Queensboro Bridge to that melancholy flute—over and over again, which is what I did. There was something so soothing about it, like it had the power to make me remember being a child. The night before, I told him, I'd gone with John to something called a drone mass at the Met's Temple of Dendur, and that had conjured a similar feeling. How it punctured something in me, bringing me to the cusp of weeping. I wonder, writing this, if what I'm after in art is a series of moods or textures. Perhaps that's all writing is now, my correspondent replies. A way to exist and process existence. It's been years since I've been out to see music, I now realize. That concert at the Met must have been the last time.

Across the street lives the man in pain. In the early evening, when the windows are open, I can hear him cry out. It comes in heartbreaking waves, and sometimes continues throughout the night. Genet and I both listen to him when all else is quiet, like we are one body, moved and disturbed. I realize that it's always warm outside when I hear him, because the windows are open. That summer, I began smoking again, after having quit for over a decade, and I would hear him when I sat outside on the porch at night. I think he's in the unit where I can see the TV set on, usually the mute heads and running scroll of CNN. I stare at the blue glow of the window. I imagine he is in a hospital bed. I don't know whether the crying out is automatic, or a result of being changed or moved.

I began smoking again after we saw the stray kitten hit by one of the speeding cars on the corner. The car didn't even slow down. I began screaming and couldn't stop shaking and screaming, until a man walking by with his three young children asked me to calm down. For the rest of the day we worried over what to do with the kitten's tiny dead body, until we called for the city to come clear it away. We've now done this several times, for cats who have been killed crossing that particular patch of street.

I know I'm not doing well when I get too caught up in the solitary lives of stray animals. This is another thing that's changed for me, being here, in the city. I feel too much for all the stray animals, yet I do almost nothing about it. It is the intensity of my concern for them that alarms me. While walking to dinner in our neighborhood that summer, we saw a large gray-white dog. She was emaciated and disoriented standing in the middle of the street, as if stuck. It didn't seem like she was aware of us. We didn't know what to do when we saw the dog, limping and confused. We stood in the middle of the street to try to shield her from oncoming cars driving too fast down the block. We didn't touch her, because we were afraid she might bite us. We thought perhaps I could go home and get food and a blanket, or we could herd the dog slowly back to our house, but what we'd do when we were there we didn't know. Home was several blocks away and the dog was barely walking. John took a photo of the dog with his phone, which we sent to our dog walker, thinking she could help. The way the dog's white fur glowed in the dark in the photograph made her look like a ghost dog. We asked people on the street if they lived nearby and could bring out food or water. I remember at the time I felt aware that this seemed like a con. Something in the urgency and mania of our requests immediately made us look suspect. Most didn't stop, but two men brought out a bowl of water. The dog took a sip. I don't know how long we stood there in the middle of the street with the dog. Suddenly a young man was beside us, or perhaps he was more like a boy. This was his dog, he told us. I asked him why she was so emaciated, gesturing to her protruding rib cage, which, I realized, came out like an accusation. She was very old, he said. We didn't realize until then that of course the dog was old, although we still didn't understand how the dog escaped, what she was doing in the middle of the street. We then stroked the dog's flank to say goodbye, as we showed affection to other dogs in the neighborhood. I was unwilling to part with her. Thinking back, I feel ashamed that I didn't touch the dog immediately, comforting her, as she was most likely dying. The young man then lifted the dog in his arms, easily, as if she weighed nothing, and carried her inside the house across the street. He didn't thank us—although what would he have thanked us for? We hadn't done anything, except perhaps make sure she wasn't hit by a car. The event unsettled both of us—there was something that didn't feel right about it. Although, thinking of the three times I have experienced the death of someone in my family, the process of witnessing a body shut down, become resistant to water or food, I remember always feeling how both natural and unreal it all felt, like something fraudulent was occurring.

Later I realized how much the dog looked like the Peter Hujar photograph, of the white dog in a field of dirt, that I had been thinking about for some time. Something so sorrowful and stripped about both of these dogs. Hujar would spend time with his animal subjects before taking their photographs so that they would relax around him. There is an aspect of time contained in these photographs, of intimacy and endurance. He captures something of their pure being. When I think of the ghost dog, my mind also goes to the old sleeping dog in Albrecht Dürer's *Melencolia I*, seemingly emaciated, the definition of the ribs.

That story of young Rilke encountering the apparition of a monk in hooded black begging for alms while staying at a spa in Viareggio frequented by the Italian royal family. Then, on the veranda, he sees the family dog, a usually friendly dachshund, who that day does not allow himself to be petted. Only later did he discover that the small dog had been kicked in the head earlier that day by a horse and was already dead, yet still upright. He wondered later whether the dog also had seen the apparition of the monk. Rilke always attributed his sensitivity to the paranormal to his mother's religiosity. The confusion over whether the little dog was still alive calls to mind the eighth of the poet's famous elegies— how, when nearing the pure space of death, one's gaze becomes like an animal's.

All summer and fall I feel obsessed and possessed by a room of Sarah Charlesworth photographs I kept returning to at the New Museum. The privacy and opacity of Charlesworth's *Stills* series, her photographs of photographs taken by others of bodies falling or jumping from buildings, captured in midair. She repurposed the photographs from other images, rephotographed and cropped them, blew them up until they are almost abstractions. Even though most of the fourteen *Stills* are from 1980, they uncannily anticipate the images of people jumping from the twin towers. Transfixed in the space, I returned again and again, photographing the images with my phone—photographing a photograph of a photograph. When I first saw the pictures, with Clutch and Jackson, who were visiting, and John, they all left the room immediately, repelled while I was mesmerized. These floating images, between life and death. Their lack of context: Unidentified woman. Unidentified man. To stand in front of an image, to feel its many layers and interpretations. Who originally took these photographs, and why?

In late August I take a photograph of a bright green praying mantis clinging to the outside of the house that looks like it's suspended in midair, just like Charlesworth's photo *Patricia Cawlings, Los Angeles*, the fifteen-year-old girl who leaped twenty feet from the roof of a Zen mission house and survived.

I am learning to see, Malte Laurids Brigge says.

On the porch one day I accidentally smash a large moth with my bare foot. The exquisite fragility of its wing, like the background of a medieval tapestry. I remember reading that some moths only live for a single day, after spending most of their life in a larval form. To live only this one day, to flutter out into the world to breed, only to be smashed instead by a dirty, naked foot. A meditation on its one day of life, like an On Kawara date painting. Today is the one day I was alive, in this form. I think about this, the dead insect like a poem, and then attempt to flick it away with the same foot, smearing its guts all over the rotted wood of the porch.

The beauty and relief of summer, Suzanne writes to me. It's painful, in a way, its power and brevity.

In September I have to go out into the world again, lengthy commutes to the various colleges and universities where I teach writing. I always forget the melancholy of the fall, when my time is not my own. All summer I had felt so hermetic, and now to return to dealing with names, with New York. My class does not fill up at the college upstate, prompting the annual panic that I might not be hired again, and so I must trudge through various trains on Labor Day to be interviewed by more prospective students, who are sometimes surprised to learn that I have published books, if I tell them or they ask, which is not often. I want to feel like I did in the summer—that space of contemplation. Not so bitter and alienated and exhausted. Where I sometimes don't feel in the shape of a person. And yet, with all of this, this ghostliness, I'm brought even closer somehow to what I desire out of the work.

There is one student at the college that semester, a freshman, kind of jangly, with rather haunted eyes, who tells me he just spent his first week here combing through VHS tapes in the library and found one of Susan Sontag interviewing Agnès Varda. Later he quotes to me that line from *The Beaches of Agnès*: "If we opened people up, we'd find landscapes."

At this college I occupy the same dim attic office as the previous fall, in one of their quaint ivy-walled houses. Every semester I feel like an impostor, temporarily occupying the spaces of tenured writers on sabbatical—as if I am temporarily occupying their lives. The office is sweltering, and I send multiple emails until a maintenance worker delivers a fan. All day, while at her desk, I glance at the professor's small wooden bookshelf of essays, presumably the texts she teaches. While waiting for students, I flip through her book of autobiographical nonfiction that also lives on the shelf, which includes her famous *New Yorker* essay. I love in the essay the detailed description of her caretaking for her dying and incontinent dog. I'm always looking for descriptions of this tenderness humans feel for their animals. I am supposedly teaching "the essay" this semester as well. On the writer's shelf the expected names, mostly male and relevant decades ago. My students all tell me they want to be one of two women writers. The names they use change every semester—but I find there are always only two.

Writing this, I am reminded of the bookstore scene in *The Walk*, when the narrator interrogates a bookseller about a bestselling book on one of the tables in that Walser way, outwardly servile, yet inwardly seething or at least aware of the absurdity:

"Could you swear that this is the most widely distributed book of the year?"

"Without a doubt!"

"Could you insist that this is the book which absolutely one has to have read?"

"Unconditionally."

"Is this book definitely good?"

"An utterly superfluous and completely inadmissible question!"

The year before, in that same office, I had repeatedly found pornography on the desktop of the shared computer. Seeing the pop-ups of naked women in various postures, I initially wondered whether they were left there by the other instructor I shared the space with when I was not on campus. Perhaps it was her research, as she was a sociologist, one of the other adjunct faculty who everyone assumes is more permanent than we are. The images were the sort of pornography that seemed designed for men who hate women. I imagined in turn that she was also suspicious, or curious, about me. I wonder if, as a resident of this city—and a partial resident of the city that is the internet—I have become almost numb to absurd or hostile encounters. I did wonder later whether the joke was on me specifically, if this pornography was left there for me, but that would take some awareness of me, or what I had written about. I never figured out if it was a form of targeted or general harassment, or what—masturbatory carelessness?

I finally said something to the woman who worked in the office downstairs, an awkward conversation I tried to laugh my way through. We were asked to lock the office afterward, and the password to the desktop was reset.

When the French sociologist (she was French) was told, she apparently just made a face of distaste, I imagine in a very French way, and asked if there were antibacterial wipes we could use to wipe down the computer and the desk, since we both ate our lunches there. Which, upon hearing this, I felt was the right reaction—and wondered why I hadn't thought of that.

There are so many bugs in the attic office. All sorts. Spiders. Lazy houseflies. Hard-shelled crawling things. They are everywhere, on the windows, around the desk, zizzing the old IKEA floor lamp with the broken dimmer. I usually leave the bugs alone, but my students become distracted by them. Sometimes I will kill one, especially if it is too loud, or crawling too close to me, or if a student looks at me expectantly. Yet my killing is random and occasional, and perhaps in that way more terrifying.

I once wrote a notebook about all of this—the office, the pornography, the reading of Walser, the bugs—for a prestigious poetry magazine that had solicited work from me. I kept on receiving edits about it throughout the previous fall, removing the bugs, then the pornography, then everything about Walser. I felt they wanted from me something else, and I couldn't give it to them. So I pulled the piece that winter. Which felt like the narrator in *The Tanners*, who wanders from job to job, quitting everything, even after only a day.

A crowded train at the beginning of the month. I am heading to a meeting for part-time faculty at the university, the only meeting we will have all semester, where a lawyer will advise us, rather hesitantly, against "improper relations with students," and when we must report anything amiss. The students' depression is not our problem, we are also told. It is probably not a good idea to have a relationship with a student, the lawyer concludes, rather indistinctly. I talk about this with Clutch, who received a similarly perplexing missive from their department in Chicago where they are teaching on a two-year contract. Who would want to fuck their student? How gross, we both agreed. Maybe the feminists in us have won out over our enthrallment to queer theory, the formlessness of Foucault's mentor-mentee relationship. On the train I help a group of Italian tourists find the correct stop for the university. They get off too early anyway. I make friendly eye contact with the other New Yorker who was helping them. She then picks up a newspaper someone threw on the seat and shows me the front page. An enlarged photograph of the drowned three-year-old Kurdish child washed up on a beach. So sad, she says, looking for my reaction. I don't say anything. I, too, feel disturbed this week reading about the migrant transport to Turkey, Greece, Germany, elsewhere, my feeling of paralysis and futility—but I do not have the language to talk about this photograph with a stranger on the train. I remember seeing Bouchra Khalili's video portrait project the previous summer, where she documented the clandestine travels of migrants wishing to enter Europe, through the recorded voiceover of their narration, the video showing only their hands drawing their journey on a map synced with their telling of it. I stood there in front of each projection, put on each set of headphones, and viewed each one, feeling a presentness I don't often feel in art spaces, or anywhere, anymore. It was one of the most affecting experiences I've had with art since I moved here.

Writing this now, copying it from my notes, I wonder at the connection between my horror and despair when looking at the photograph of the dead Kurdish child, and my fascination with Sarah Charlesworth's floating bodies. Just that week, I had shown a student Peter Hujar's photograph of Candy Darling, her languid pose on her deathbed, the white hospital sheets wrapped around her like an evening gown, and wondered later whether I should have given some sort of warning first. Although Candy Darling was not dead but dying, as were many of Sarah Charlesworth's subjects, imminently.

Should I give a date here? September 15. The same date
that opens May Sarton's journal. Commuting through
crowds again. On the way home, everyone is asleep on
the train, hunched over, exhausted, or pretending to be
asleep so they don't have to give up their seat. The choking feeling in my chest has returned—something like
radiant despair. Like I could collapse at any time and
begin weeping. The porousness and permeability of this
heat. I am beginning to see twins everywhere. On the
train, the two little sisters in matching white cardigans
with silver sequins playing with each other's clothes.
Dressed alike, as my sister and I were as children. Their
mother next to them, exhausted, a warm hand with yellowing nails reaching across two pairs of thin legs. How
Sebald once told his students that when in doubt, bring
twins into the narrative. There is always a moment for
me, in the heat, in this city, where I begin to unravel.
After class I meet John in Midtown for lunch, but I have
no appetite. I stop on 42nd Street, outside the library,
where a man displays animals on a blanket—birds in a
cage, rabbits, a dog, a couple cats. Tourists take photographs, like they're watching an amusing sideshow. I
push to the front of the crowd. Do they have water? I
demand. A police car pulls up, does nothing. Yet I really

do nothing. I am far too selfish. I can only handle one psychotic terrier, who disrupts my nerves daily. I don't want to be David Lurie in Coetzee's *Disgrace*, taking on the task of euthanizing the dogs that no one wants. David Lurie with his old masters and old ways. At the university, I take a photo of a mailbox labeled David Lurie, belonging to a professor of East Asian languages. In the cluttered communal room, I notice a copy of *Disgrace*, as if Coetzee's professor character is haunting me. When I feel exposed like this, I begin to make connections with everything—I see literature everywhere, a vast referentiality. *You are not David Lurie!* I write in my notebook.

At the end of September, a prominent writer of so-called autofiction, with a half-million-dollar advance on his last book, wins the so-called genius grant. All day, friends contact me to complain. This writer's name had become synonymous for the type of first-person narrative we also wrote, and yet no one found our struggles worthy of reward. Why do these prizes and awards only seem to breed more prizes and awards? Yes, something about breeding, something I didn't quite grasp. Maybe our work was too much about acknowledging failure, about doubt. But ours was a community of doubt. We saw something beautiful and comradely in our doubt. Maybe prize committees prize confidence, the ooze of it. I wanted to know, how did this writer have the confidence to write his novel seemingly in real time, over a year? When we take years just thinking and taking notes? This was a philosophical concern for me, as well as a complaint. The problem with the work I was writing was one of time. The present tense was a problem for me. And yet I wanted my novel, if that's what it was, to be about time and the problem of time. Amina writes me, about the novel she is attempting to write, the desire to write both the *full* and the *fleeting* sensations. How to capture that? The problem with dailiness—how to write the day when it escapes us. It was the problem at the center of the work I was trying to write, although I was unsure whether I was really trying to write it. Never have I felt more emptied of the possibility of writing but more full of it at the same time. When did I realize I was suffering not from writer's block but from refusal?

In yoga class, everyone goes around and gives their "fall intentions." The sexy girl with the shaved head whom I sometimes fantasize about in class says she is working on kindness, and discovering that kindness to self and others can be a slow process. Two others say they're working on being comfortable with doubt and uncertainty, not pushing things, knowing they will happen. Some more "loving kindness." I pass. It always gets me how mute and inarticulate I am in these settings. I'm supposed to be a writer, yet language doesn't come easily to me, and when it does, I am suspicious of it. But I like the idea of yoga being about a practice, about not knowing. That's what writing is for me. A ritual. My impulse to write was private, was the way that I was silent, or not silent, in the face of capitalism, desire, the family. Was a way to write through these feelings.

John sends me the obituary of an art critic—a failed painter who had started painting again—because he knew I'd like it. "Although my guess is that the art 'object' is done with, I myself still go on making 'paintings,' but this doesn't have much to do with making salable physical objects. Making them is more like philosophical investigations, art criticism, or yoga."

The problem with the work I was writing was one of time. Now that I was inside the semester, I didn't have any time to write. Or, when I had the time, I didn't have the mental space. On days when I wasn't teaching, I felt so distracted, never in a pure space to think. When I feel too consumed, I also cannot read—everything feels too porous. I sit on the couch and ignore my surroundings. I surrender to screens. I read reviews of shows I don't even watch. I watch clips of actresses on talk shows, the repetitive gesture of them smoothing their hair behind their ears, their rehearsed anecdote, their bashful or witty humility, their glowing skin, their charming white teeth. Open on my laptop, amidst other windows, I watch Hitchcock's *Vertigo* over and over, just like the narrator in Chris Marker's *Sans Soleil*, his meditation on memory.

Can you think of writing as a gaze? I ask my students, who are mostly unmoved. This is what I wished for in writing—a gaze that was elegiac and hungover. Clutch writes me of the trance they go into now when they are teaching. All the mindless things I bleat out about the essay. My performance has grown thinner and thinner. I feel we are supposed to be sages when teaching writing,

I complain to Clutch, that's what the students want—to tell them not only how to write from life but also how to live. When I have not figured out how to live. On the couch, paging through the photos of Roland Barthes, captioned "Distress: lecturing" and "Boredom: a panel discussion," in *Roland Barthes by Roland Barthes*. When I write Danielle about this, she says she was also on her couch, on that same day, staring at the same page.

It was that fall that Chantal Akerman died. She had committed suicide. Some believed she was in despair over her last film being booed at a festival, a film that takes place almost entirely in her elderly mother's Brussels apartment before her mother's death, a film Akerman edited while still deep in grief. I was trying again to find a publisher for a book I'd written about my mother, and was in the process of receiving a fresh round of rejections. I meant to write "round," but originally I wrote "wound." The life of an artist seems so exquisitely sad sometimes, I wrote to Bhanu, when I learned about Akerman's death. How fragile it can feel, when an artist commits suicide. And so I thought of Akerman's films all fall. How her work was so brilliant at recording dead time and blank space. That is all I want a work of art to do, to record time, to imagine other vast solitudes, including our own. My cinephile student and I mourn Akerman together. We are both rewatching her films. The slow silence of *Hotel Monterey*, that beautiful shot of the pregnant woman in the hallway like a Vermeer. That desire I feel, for art that is like a trance. I tell my student I have been watching clips of *Sans Soleil* on my phone, while riding on the train through the Hudson River Valley.

I try to make it outside on the porch with Genet so he can enjoy the autumn sun. The landlord has cut back the butterfly bush. I am bleeding heavily. Dreams of blood now mark time for me. I get home and the dog has scattered my bloody tampons and pads all around the living room but mostly immediately in front of the door. The little presents he leaves for me—*How dare you abandon me!* At community acupuncture, I get a painful needle in the center palm for sleep, as I haven't been sleeping well. I've been having trouble closing the border between day and night. I am woken up by my upstairs neighbor knocking on my door, telling me she just caught a kid urinating in our backyard and trying to steal my bicycle. He ran away. We stand in the entryway, marinating in the excitement. I admired her wool poncho—I spend all fall coveting everyone's fall coats. I googled her the other day: She takes Nan Goldin–esque photographs, everyone naked in bed in blissed-out orgies and stoned, half-closed eyes. I never see her. I am continually confused by who now lives upstairs. Their constant deliveries I sign for, while Genet has fits. There is the agoraphobic self-help guru who tells me in passing that she just ordered fountain pens from Japan. I suppose she tells me because she'd heard I was a writer, or perhaps she just saw me writing in my notebook on the porch. There is the blond actress with imaginary bedbugs who is in the bedroom directly above ours—we can hear her take apart her bed at night. She is often away, acting in regional theater.

My father visits in early October. All we have in common is old films. Together we can go into various arcana of early Hollywood. At night on the couch in his basement he watches one of his vast collection of John Wayne movies. That night we watch *The Philadelphia Story* together, him uncomfortable on the couch, Genet trying to hump his arm, me sitting on the floor. We share a love for Jimmy Stewart, his second favorite actor after John Wayne, I think because they were both Reagan Republicans. I can see my father is not well. He is frail, his belly has gotten massive. He pees all over my bathroom floor.

My notes for the last time I watched *Vertigo*:

"Do you believe that someone out of the past, someone dead, can enter into possession of a living being?"

"She wanders. God knows she wanders."

"Anyone could become obsessed with the past."

On September 11, 1902—the same date will begin his
novel—Rilke writes a letter to Rodin, in his halting
French, recalling an earlier conversation. He had told
the old man that his wife was coming to Paris to work,
and so must leave their daughter with her grandparents.
The sculptor had replied, *Oui, il faut travailler, rien que
travailler*. Rilke's desire to learn from the sculptor, to
adopt his mode of being, echoed throughout his life in
his search for masters to tell him how to occupy his time.
He took Rodin's advice as gospel, repeating it to him almost a year later in this letter: I must learn to work, to
work, he repeats, that is where I fall so short! He reminds
the sculptor of his statement and tells him that he'd come
to Paris not only to write a study of his work but also to
ask him: How was one to live? And now he understands,
the young poet writes to the sculptor. To work is to live
without dying. But how to find the quiet space inside
himself within which to work? This will occupy him for
many years. The frightening abyss that opens up between his good days. The sculptor suggests he study the
zoo animals at the Jardin des Plantes, as he himself once
did. Rilke writes his famous poem about the panther's
exhausted gaze through the bars of his prison. More than
a decade later, in the midst of crisis, unsure whether he

should still write, exhausted after finishing his novel, he tells Lou Andreas-Salomé of a dream of a pale lion in a freshly painted green cage, and within the same cage a naked man, seemingly on exhibition. Over the pallor of the man's nude flesh, and over the dream, a violet shadow. (She tells him that his dream is of Paris, that he must return.) When Clara comes to Paris, they barricade themselves inside their separate studios and take the sculptor's dictum literally, seeing each other only on Sundays. Miserable in their closed-off spaces, they despise Paris, its dreary winter. The cruelty and confusion of the streets, the beauty one can find in the art here, does not replace the monstrosity, Rilke writes to one of their friends on New Year's Day.

Once the book on the sculptor is finished, Rilke does not know how to occupy his time. He writes in a letter that the city has plotted against his attempts to stay inside and write, its unrelenting scream has broken against his silence, its fearsomeness follows him into his sad room. This catalyzes three attacks of influenza—long feverish nights shot through with dread, just like the great fevers of his childhood. Finally, after the third attack of flu, his father gives him money to recover in solitude again at the Italian shore. Exhausted, in the midst of a severe depression, he swims nude in the ocean, eats only fruit and milk, and attempts work on some poems.

Later in the fall, as the weather changes, I begin traveling by myself into the city on my days off, to walk around aimlessly, to turn time into space. My walks that fall were the opposite of the impulse to search for my name online, to see whether I still existed. I am reminded of that line of Sontag's: "For the character born under the sign of Saturn, time is the medium of constraint, inadequacy, repetition, mere fulfillment. In time, one is only what one is: what one has always been. In space, one can be another person." On one such Saturday I feel compelled to leave—to disappear. I dress simply—white button-down, black jeans, black plain sneakers, my floor-grazing black coat with its various folds. I love how the coat makes me feel strange, exorbitant, but worry today that I am too conspicuous. Today I just want to be lost. To be someone other than myself. There is a bereftness to waiting for the train to go into the city on an overcast Saturday. Couples in puffer coats cling to each other. I like to look at what's been thrown onto the tracks: a Play-Doh container, a plastic hanger, mini plastic rum bottles. On the train I don't want to write in my notebook, because I don't wish to be conspicuous, but I do anyway. It is boring to look at people on this train, everyone on their phones. A pair of young women with

identical looks—glittering black sneakers, immaculate
makeup they check on their phones, dark shiny jeans.
One glares at me, as if annoyed, either at my coat or that
I'm writing in my notebook. I become so self-conscious
as she stares that I stop and close my eyes. On the train
I try to read my book of stories, a Walser collection I'd
just received in the mail, but I can only flip through it.
The introduction is by William Gass. Lately it seems that
every book I'm reading has an introduction by William
Gass or Susan Sontag. I underline two lines: "At least
three of Walser's seven siblings were successful. Success was something Walser studied, weighed, admired,
mocked, refused." Anna was just emailing me, worried
that she should be online more, interacting with readers,
so that she's not forgotten. Lately I just want to shrink
as small as possible. To write as small as possible. That
is the space of my longing, however irrational. I watch
a girl apply mascara, sandwiched between two women
in puffy coats who get off at Canal Street. While standing to exit at Union Square, I take a photograph on my
phone of my favorite psychic flyer.

KEANO

SPIRITUAL CONSULTANT

POWERFUL MASTER IN LOVE

TELLS PAST-PRESENT-FUTURE

After the number, it offers one free question by phone. If
I had one free question, what would I ask? The thought
preoccupies me as I sit writing up my notes in a crowded

coffee shop on Avenue A—the only place I've found where I can sit and write—while a family crowds in next to me, the boys talking of video games. As I walk around, feeling irritated, crushed, by the crowds of brunchgoers, my aimlessness begins to feel soothing for me. In my notebook, a quote I ripped from a lamppost, finding it perversely funny: "People rarely succeed unless they have fun in what they are doing."—Dale Carnegie. How easily, I write in my notebook, the day can escape. How difficult it can be to attempt to penetrate it, to describe the texture of what it means to walk around in a body. After some time I find I can block out the voices around me, can begin to write in a way that feels like walking around, can try to write what I'm thinking. I want to know what it's like to be a psychic, to feel such porousness, is it painful? Or, if the psychic is pretending to be psychic, what is it like being an impostor? While walking around I take pictures of psychic signs in shop windows. The glowing cursive handwriting. The small hominess of the window display, the few crystals, the table. Since I moved here, I keep taking photographs of these signs. They make me feel calm, radiant. At Tompkins Square, the dog parade is just letting out. The dogs seem so cheerful in their costumes. I try to take a picture of a pack of them. The Doberman in the massive purple tutu, the little terrier dressed as a cardboard box of Dove soap, a hamburger dog, a painting-easel dog, a pumpkin dog, a rat terrier with just X's in orange masking tape covering his flank. All fall I think about the opening narration of *Sans Soleil*, the trance of the female voice: "He

wrote, 'I've been round the world several times, and now
only banality still interests me. On this trip, I've tracked
it with the relentlessness of a bounty hunter.'" The bat-
teries fall out of my camera into the street, and I must
scramble to scoop them up. As I attempt to fit them back
in, I eavesdrop on a man covered from bald head to
toe in tattoos, talking to two women—about someone,
assumedly at the parade, wearing an outfit that costs more
than he makes in a month. As I hear this I feel embarrassed of my conspicuous black coat. Walking around,
I feel crushed by all the crowds. I see an older woman
in a bowler hat and bright red hair, head to toe black,
a rainbow cane, her little dog. I smile at her gratefully.
I continue to wander around, down Avenue A. Outside
a medical supplies store, a sign: a smiling woman inside
an MRI machine, with the words ARE YOU CLAUS-
TROPHOBIC? The storefront of an old photocopier
repair store makes me think of Sebald and Cornell, how
they didn't take their own photos but sometimes copied
found photos inside a photostat. I remember now that
I had wanted to write about Joseph Cornell during the
fall, about how I had begun seeing landscapes through
his vision. I go inside a kitschy odditorium, with Ouija
boards, various creepy things, a glass case with empty
nineteenth-century medicinals. I think of Diane Arbus
visiting odditoriums near Times Square. A sign tells customers not to pet the horned stuffed calf. This is some
Edgar Allan Poe shit, says a drunk man asking to use
the bathroom. I listen to him and the pink-haired girl behind the counter argue over whether Edgar Allan Poe

lived in New York or Baltimore. New York, he said, but she said he was wrong. I almost intervened, thinking of Poe's tiny cottage in the Bronx, where he lived during the last years of his life, the caged songbirds on the front porch, how he would write poems with his cat on his shoulder. The manager asks the man to leave. This used to be more of a colorful neighborhood, but there are still colorful characters, he says in an ingratiating way to a tourist family. I am reminded again of *Sans Soleil*, the scene of drunken homeless men in Japan. "He didn't like to dwell on poverty." A few blocks away, I find myself inside Mast Books. I flip through Nan Goldin's *Ballad of Sexual Dependency* on the table, which I keep on paging through whenever I find it in a bookstore. I marvel again at the vulnerability, and yet formal elegance, of this series of portraits of bodies and community and time. The way Goldin indexes images. The stiff pose of her parents next to a pair of mannequins. The intimacy of photographing her friends in solitude. Alone looking at a bathroom mirror. Naked while sad or voluptuous in bed. Showering or in a bath. Weeping or masturbating. The rawness of the self-portraits, the brutality of the artist's battered face, her heart-shaped bruise. The starkness of emotions. Her tribe, so many of them no longer here. Cookie Mueller bored in a bar. Greer Lankton. A study in couples and pairs. In party dresses. Embracing naked. Goldin and her ex Brian posed in bed, like a watchful theater. I trace my hand across the spines of the vintage Grove editions. I pick up a New Directions translation of Roberto Bolaño's *Antwerp*, because it has on the back, in gold embossing, "The only novel that doesn't embarrass me is Antwerp," the only book I buy and take home with me. How much I understand that sentiment—although every book I've published embarrasses me. With both their visibility and their invisibility. How I now feel slightly paranoid in bookstores, how being an author has changed my relationship to them. Now that I look for Walser, I see they don't have my books, a fact I greet with fleeting ambivalence. I finger a copy of Cioran's *The Trouble with Being Born*. An old copy of Jean Rhys's *Good Morning, Midnight* with a terrible moony illustration of a woman on the cover. I take a photograph of a facsimile of one of Basquiat's notebook pages, which I'd just seen on exhibit at the Brooklyn Museum: *I feel like a citizen it's time to go and come back a drifter.* After watching the Julian Schnabel biopic of Basquiat sometime that fall, I had emailed Anna, wondering whether the drive to fame is something like the drive to genius. Basquiat wanted to be famous. And he was. But he was also a genius. I used to dismiss so many artists who wanted fame—but then the ones who want fame are the ones who are remembered, more often than not. Like Robert Mapplethorpe, who played the game, unlike Peter Hujar, who did not. I wonder sometimes about my identification with writers and artists who were failures. Anna wrote back that yes, in a person's lifetime, the successful ones are the ones who want to be, who are in the right place in the right time with the right look and the right agent and the right personality, but after we're all dead, she thought, it's anyone's game who's remembered. Which of course is how she would think about it, as a competition, still, even after death. Anna was always worried about being remembered. That was her ambition, to be remembered. I wasn't sure anyone was going to be remembered. Writing was what I felt compelled to do while I was living. Not about what would happen after I was dead. Maybe writing was about being visible when I felt invisible, as I felt invisible as a child, unspecial, ignored. Or maybe writing was about becoming invisible again after having become too visible. Maybe it was both. I wasn't sure anymore. A genius goes inside someone else's heart and blood and stays there forever, Anna wrote me. Maybe this was the difference between the two of us. Anna was sure we were geniuses, or at least sure that she was. I was worried that I was a fraud. That's what publishing a book felt like—that every book was somehow an elaborate fraud, and I would someday be found out.

The evening makes everything slightly sinister. People walk around with pointy ears, even though Halloween is still two weeks away. Every other man is dressed as Spider-Man. I wander around a flea market housed outside an old church. There is junk everywhere, glassware, boxes of nail polish. They are packing up. I flip through photographs of unidentified people in a box, combing through unknown smiling faces, the banality and pain of their lives lost to me. Unidentified family photographs in a junk-store bin would be on my "lists that quicken the heart," just like Sei Shōnagon's in *The Pillow Book*,

which the filmmaker narrator in *Sans Soleil* borrows as
his criterion for what he films. It is getting late. I walk
toward Union Square. A man lying in the window
recess of a large bank waves at me, and he does it in so
charming a way that I wave back and go over to him. I
give him money and mention that it's going to be cold
tonight. I linger, wanting to talk. I wonder why I don't
take off wandering more. I consider, could I just completely choose to leave my identity, my name, to become
someone else? I go into a gay bar near Union Square. It
is nearly empty inside, decorated with cobwebs, a few
men in groups. I was here the previous year, for a birthday party for a well-known editor who had just edited
an anthology I appeared in. It was at that party that I'd
met a famous writer whose short stories made me want to
become a writer when I read them in my early twenties.
The writer looked like she did in her photographs, like
a wonderful and spooky blond ostrich. I finally went up
to her, at the end of the night, and told her how much
her work meant to me. I knew that I was bothering
her, that she would have probably rather I had left her
alone. She kept on telling me how bad her new book
was, how afraid she was of having it published, how it
was not ready, how she shouldn't have written it. It's not
good, she kept on repeating. It's just not good. I did that
thing with her I do to most women in my life, where I
soothe them, become sycophantic. It is wonderful I'm
sure, I said to her. It will be great. Everyone will love
it. I remember feeling that she knew that I was full of it,

and wishing I could have acted in a different way. That perhaps she was in turn watching me with the cruelty of one of her characters, observing my blathering. I sit at the bar and write up my notes from my walk in my notebook. Next to me, a man wearing high-waisted jeans, a black turtleneck, and a flashlight as a necklace is watching a film on his laptop. He resembles Steve Jobs, and only typing up my notes now do I realize that this may have been his costume. Are you a writer? he asks me. Yes, I reluctantly answer. I always dread that question and the possible conversation that follows. What genre? he asks. I tell him I never really know how to answer that. Like fictional novels? he asks. In a way, yes, I say to him. Would I write down my name so he can look it up later? For some reason I write down the name that was not my name, that I'd written inside the cover of my yellow notebook. He folds up the piece of paper in an exacting way, opening his leather attaché case. I then ask him whether he is editing something. He looks so intent with his headphones on. No, he works in crisis management. Like after 9/11, he says to me, as if that was an explanation. He tells me he is watching *The Man Who Would Be King*, which I look up later, a seventies Technicolor starring Sean Connery and Michael Caine, an adaptation of a Rudyard Kipling story set in a nineteenth-century colonialist India. It seems the exact sort of Orientalist fantasy my father would love. He watches it once a day, he says to me. I tell him I haven't seen it. I write in a notebook too, he tells me. He takes out a diary, from a pocket of his briefcase seemingly designed for this purpose. It was one of those small diaries that my father keeps in his widowed solitude, to note errands each day. He hands it to me, and, not knowing what else I am supposed to do, I flip through it. It is completely blank.

On the day before Halloween I take the train into the city to walk through Midtown. More people in costumes at Herald Square. The blank uniformity of the twin mannequins with orange hair in the window at Macy's. Everything again takes on an odd cast. I want to visit the Webster Apartments, the all-women residence where I stayed one year during a magazine internship in college. On the train, I look at their website on my phone. In answering a question about famous former residents, they respond that unlike the Barbizon uptown, where Sylvia Plath wrote *The Bell Jar*, they are not aware of any famous people who lived there, but if they knew the names of their former residents, they are sure their success stories would fill volumes, a formulation that amuses me. Walking up toward Penn Station, I find myself entering the Kmart I remember from twenty years ago. I seem to be in a fugue state, riding up the escalators to every floor. I realize then that I regularly have dreams of wandering around this same Kmart. In my dream there is a photo booth on the bottom floor, near the exit to Penn Station, although when I get to the bottom floor the photo booth is not there. I must have wandered around for at least an hour. I remember my mother buying our clothes at such stores when I was a child, which might explain the fascination and horror I feel for them now. When I was a twenty-year-old intern, I maxed out a credit card trying to buy clothes that would make me blend in here, all the shops on Canal, blazer and skirt outfits. And then when I moved here, drawn to all the beautiful conformity, that desire to look New York enough, to wear the right thing. Elizabeth Hardwick writes in *Sleepless Nights*: "From shame I have paid attention to clothes, shoes, rings, watches, accents, teeth, points of deportment, turns of speech." I remember a line from a negative review of my last book: how suspicious the reviewer was of glamour, how she felt glamour was an empty suit. But what about Walser's dandyism, I now want to respond. His shabby three-piece suits of reds, yellows, and blues, his rolled-up trousers. That photograph of Kafka as a young law student, his English bowler hat, frock coat, and stiff collar, like Flaubert's Frédéric in *Sentimental Education*, Kafka's favorite novel. His father's fancy goods store sold gloves, along with haberdashery, parasols, umbrellas, walking sticks, silk handkerchiefs, silk ribbons, scarves, lace, buttons, slippers, fans, jewelry, and elegant decorative objects and knickknacks made of cast iron, bronze, zinc, silver, leather, wood, ivory, glass, lead. My desire now is not to look like everyone else, but like a dandy, like Baudelaire. Somehow conspicuous and also invisible. The rows of Christmas teddy bears stare at me as I descend the escalator at the Kmart. The dreamlike scenes in the Tokyo department store in *Sans Soleil*. The filmmaker reflects on an intense love for anonymous inhabitants of a city. "I begin to wonder if those dreams are really mine, or if they're part of a totality, a giant collective dream." That scene too in *Wanda*, Barbara Loden walking around the department store as if in a trance, staring at a mannequin, the two women, at least one unreal. I wander around the picked-over costumes section. I take a photograph of a $9.99 mask, with a shredded veil over it. Skulls and cobwebs. Cat skeletons. Another photo of a ghost costume, a cheap white plastic hooded robe. I suddenly remember my brother as a child, maybe five years old, crying on the front steps on Halloween day, as we posed for pictures before school. In my memory I do not know why he is crying. Perhaps he did not want to go as a clown again. We were always clowns. My mother made those costumes on her sewing machine, and so every year we were the same trio of clowns. The three of us children only one year apart, the smallest in our classes, too smart for our own good, especially my brother, the one considered the genius, yet all of us tiny, oversensitive, and intense. Never store-bought costumes. Too expensive. I don't remember why my brother was crying, only that he was. It is always around Halloween that I feel most haunted by my mother, that I viscerally revisit learning that she was dying. I eventually leave the Kmart and wander into the Webster. It's exactly the same, like it's still trapped in the 1950s. The intense familiarity of the salmon-colored walls, the pay phones in little chambers. When I ask if I can go upstairs, the security guard tells me only residents are allowed in the rooms. While looking through these notes my mind keeps floating not to the scene of the Webster

but to Chantal Akerman's *Hotel Monterey*, the silent long
takes inside the SRO, saturated with the sadness and solitude of a Hopper painting . . . I read somewhere it's now
a Days Inn. Like a voiceover over these stills, I think of
Elizabeth Hardwick's portraits of the transients and
drifters living at the Hotel Schuyler in *Sleepless Nights*.
While writing this I find a postcard online for the Hotel
Schuyler, "A Home Away from Home," off Fifth Avenue
and Radio City, rooms, suites, apartments with or without kitchenettes. Air-conditioned. I used to walk to my
Time magazine internship from 34th Street to the Time
Warner building across from Radio City. I would sit in
my little unwatched cubicle and use the communal
printer to print out pages of my bad play that I was trying
to write, then wander home through Times Square at
night. At the diner across the street from the Webster I
sit on one of the vinyl silver glitter stools at the counter,
staring at the miniature boxes of cereal lined above the
milkshake machine, the open-cut cantaloupe wrapped in
plastic, the massive pies, the goopy large strawberries
on cheesecakes. How much my mother loved to sit at a
diner counter and order a slice of pie. How those are the
only types of restaurants where we ate growing up, but
only on special occasions, like Christmas Eve. Joseph
Cornell's list of sweets in his 1946 diary, which I'm reading: "caramel pudding, a few donuts, cocoa, white bread,
peanut butter, peach jam, a milky way, some chocolate
eclairs, a half-dozen sweet buns, a peach pie, a cake with
icing, and a prune twist." I watch the waitress as she refills
my coffee, her blue baseball cap and blue apron. I feel

like I'm dressing as someone I'm not, in my leather jacket and chunky silver rings and long white tunic. The jacket I purchased when I first moved here, as a way to feel like I belonged—not the expected cropped jacket, but androgynous and tough, like Joan of Arc. How coats are always a way for me to become another person. How many years I worked in twenty-four-hour diners, the same type where we ate growing up; even now I feel like a prodigal daughter when I am back inside one. Elizabeth Hardwick writing that store clerks and waitresses were the heroines of her memories. Hardwick studied Rilke's *Notebooks of Malte Laurids Brigge* when writing her novel, and a similar decreation occurs in her work— going away from the self, preferring to tell other stories, of the washerwomen and waitresses of her youth, of the denizens of the hotel, as opposed to telling her own. Later, I watch the waitress picking through a salad at one of the small booths. I feel I can inhabit some layer of her exhaustion. I fight an intense desire to ask her if they are hiring. The ravishing desire to quit my other life, to go back to my past. But maybe the same way Jimmy Stewart in *Vertigo* quits being a detective but doesn't quit at the same time. Like Wittgenstein with philosophy. Or Walser with writing. Every time Walser moved to a new city he forgot his past. All the shabby rooming houses he lived in. His fixation with waitresses in his fiction. I think of Joseph Cornell, his obsession with Joyce Hunter, the teenage runaway from Kentucky forty years his junior who poured him coffee at the Strand Food Shop on Sixth Avenue. He gifted her little collages, which she resold. She also stole boxes from him, but he never pressed charges. She had left her husband and baby in Philadelphia to try to be an actress. He found an innocence and vulnerability in her, like his other muses of the ordinary, the working girls who ate their brown paper bag lunches at Union Square. Joyce Hunter was murdered two years after she met him, stabbed to death by a male acquaintance in an Upper West Side rooming house in 1964. The silent color film he made the following year, out of mourning, filming the Flushing Cemetery where she was buried. It was the second short film he made at the Flushing Cemetery, the first being *Angel*, mostly static shots of an angel statue and a pool, like a series of meditations, shot through with the blue of a sunny November day.

On Halloween night, holed up in the bedroom, hiding from the doorbell for the dog's sake, multiple screens open on my computer. I watch the beginning of *Sans Soleil* in a loop, transcribing the narration into my notebook— how mesmerized I feel by that form of distanced address, how I itch to copy it. The narrator recounts a letter she had received from the traveling documentarian Sandor Krasna, his thoughts on how the nineteenth century dealt with concepts of space, and the twentieth century dealt with the "coexistence of different concepts of time." I wonder in my notebook if, in the twenty-first century, we deal with layered notions of time and space. Can a work of literature contain the energy of the internet, its distracted nature?

That entire fall I had an urge to walk. How eerily warm it was, like something prophetic. On a local election day, I did not have to go into work, yet I still traveled in the rush-hour crush of bodies, hoping to spend some time flipping through books on Joseph Cornell at the Mid-Manhattan Library, despite still not having a library card. The train was late and crushed with people—I let my gaze wander over everyone crowded in one space. The day before, exhausted on the train upstate, I found myself mostly on my phone, reading recaps of the TV show I watched the previous night. I did eventually take out a copy of Sebald's *Vertigo* and let myself read the Vienna scene, which I seem to keep rereading, unable to move on. I found myself finally being able to read, and with reading, write a little, and while walking through the autumnal fire of trees up the hill to campus I let my mind wander, writing in a way. I never know, when I sit down to write, how to replicate that movement and those discoveries that come when my mind wanders. When I sit down to write, I begin to wander to another thought entirely. I think of Sebald saying in an interview that when he sat down to write, he didn't know where he was going, he followed his thoughts and connections like a dog in a field. And yet why do I love thinking about that, but dislike George's assertion that there's a mystical aspect to language? Maybe it's the loftiness I felt that some ascribe to the project of writing, as if it's some sort of higher plane of existence. Or the preciousness of it. Or, worse, the idea that writing is a form of therapy. And isn't this what we're supposed to say to students who want to be writers, as a way to tell them that writing isn't about success, or capitalism, it's personal, self-directed, sacred? Maybe I even feel that, but I resent that I'm supposed to sell it. Sell writing. Sell a life of being a writer. Was being a writer a way of escaping from having a job, or was it, as others have framed it, extreme discipline and unceasing solitary labor? I didn't know anymore. The lofty comparison irked me; the spirit of Sebald's comment is right, to write with attention to the present is in some way to become like a dog.

On the train the next day, clinging to the sweaty metal pole, I watch everyone on their phones. The red-haired woman next to me keeps swiping right or left, and I watch her nails, previously painted red or purple, still stained despite a careless swipe of nail polish remover. I become aware how torn and dirty my own fingernails are, with dried, unkempt cuticles, the way Hans Castorp views with horror his Russian beloved. Sometimes I am distracted at what women are wearing, a certain type of groomed professional woman. I would hate to be one of those women with perfect manicures, Anna writes to me. I'd want to kill myself. I didn't write back to her that I found myself wanting to imitate them when I moved here. The question of grooming continually perplexes me—how it seems so quickly to degrade. Yesterday on the train I stared at a woman's chipped, worn-down burgundy nails. Sometimes, looking at strangers asleep on the train or staring at their chipped nails, or watching them carefully apply makeup in the mirror, that tenderness feels like the only time I'm sure I am a writer.

Since the main library is not open until 10 a.m., I find myself walking to Grand Central to get my bagel and coffee, just as I had the day before. There is a difference between strolling through such a public space, with time, and the way I usually enter the station, crazed and sprinting, trying to make my train. Since taking these walks, I find myself tracing the same circumference, like Sebald's unnamed narrator in *Vertigo*, circling the same sickle-shaped area in Vienna. There are several German-looking men in Grand Central who look like Sebald with his rucksack. It's difficult in midtown Manhattan to find a space to sit, write in a notebook, and read. I finally find a small crumby table outside of the coffee stand. The old woman next to me, drinking her small coffee, scrolling through her phone. There's such a different texture to boredom now, I think. And I am more than susceptible. I check my email, I answer a few messages, I forget where I am, what I am doing. Scroll through fall coats on sale at expensive boutiques. There becomes an economics of shopping here—it's half off of extremely expensive, like half-a-month's-rent expensive. When you think about it, that's almost affordable. And anyway a coat is an investment. There's a note in the margins of my notebook from that day that I can't decipher—some research about apple cider vinegar and constipation. I find myself stuck this way at Grand Central. I go upstairs and watch from above as the tourists in the main hall gaze up at the cerulean astronomical ceiling that Joseph Cornell loved so much. Cornell observing the crowds in the Grand Central waiting room, "absorbed in coming and going of endless flow." The tourists staring up at selfie sticks like personal Eiffel Towers. I think to myself that some people take photographs as a way to not really see. I wonder if I'm one of those people, or if I take photographs as a way to pay attention, to have the tiniest window through which to look closely. I also write, in my notebook that day, about paying attention, how it is a radical act, thinking of May Sarton copying down Simone Weil's line in her journal: "Attention is prayer." Later Danielle repeats this same phrase to me, in an email.

At the library I feel vaguely misanthropic, with everyone still taking selfies inside the grand building. I am told I cannot get a library card because I forgot to bring proof of address, even though I show the man in the small gray room several up-to-date university and college faculty IDs from all of my various campuses. Apparently this is not enough proof that I live here. I sit on the floor and try to write in my notebook, but I am told by a security guard to leave. I go behind the building and sit in Bryant

Park. I want to sit here and think about *Nymphlight*, Joseph Cornell's little film set in Bryant Park, the silence and space of his ballet of pigeons, which I watched on YouTube the night before. Yet outside in Bryant Park it is all crowds, here for an ongoing winter festival sponsored by a bank. I sit and watch the carousel and try to calm down. I watch the mothers with their young children, documenting the ride on their phones, and wonder if I feel some sort of longing watching them. I like the carousel best when it goes around and around emptily to its French cabaret theme. Surely Cornell loved this carousel, I think. Strange to think that he may have sat here, on his lunch break or day off, watching the same sort of scene that I'm watching now. Our bodies in time layer over each other. Although he probably would have appeared creepier for sitting here watching children on a carousel. As the carousel goes around I see myself in the foil mirrors of its interior. Around and around, not going anywhere. Some of the butterflies on the facade are held up with duct tape. The cat with gold fingernails looks so calm, and yet surprised. When I text John where I am, he texts back that he loves the demented bunny the best. The frog is so grumpy, I reply. I watch an older well-dressed woman by herself, on the bench, riding in circles. I watch an extremely tanned mother and daughter stop outside the carousel to take selfies. They have matching long blond hair, leather miniskirts, stilettos. They take picture after picture of unsmiling faces in front of the carousel, without looking at it, scrolling through the phone to examine the resulting photographs. A little girl scoops up gravel and throws it at me, and I smile at her. Her playfulness and spontaneity calms me down. I look up Bryant Park on my phone and learn that it used to be a potter's field, that thousands of bodies of the poor or unclaimed were buried here, before being moved to Wards Island. Later there were forty miles of bookshelves underground, but now the library is being emptied of its books. I try to think of that, of all the dead bodies there before the books. And now the nothingness.

Afterward, I wander across the street to the Mid-Manhattan branch. There are no tourists here, just people sitting around, passing time, heads on the tables. Mostly men, with books open in front of them. It is so quiet. I feel more at home here, in its griminess. I go upstairs to the fifth floor to find the biography of Joseph Cornell that I wanted. I sit down at a large table and read that Cornell was a lover of biographies. "They attest at least partly to the difficulty he had in sustaining friendships. He fared better with the deceased. He loved to immerse himself in the lives of the illustrious dead, with whom his identification was intense . . ." I watch an ancient-looking man wearing a baseball cap, a red sweatshirt, a paisley scarf around his neck, eating an orange out of a plastic bag, reading a book with a magnifying glass. I sit across from a woman in a red coat and a fluorescent pink hood. She has books all around her. A book on Rasputin. One on wooden spoons. I realize she is asleep. I think back to watching Shirley Clarke's *Portrait of Jason* last week, recorded in the middle of the night from Turner

Classic Movies. I kept on pausing on Shirley Clarke's bookcase in her room in the Chelsea Hotel, while Jason Holliday ventriloquizes Katharine Hepburn's calla lilies speech from *Stage Door*. There is a skull on top of a pile of books in the background, a sort of vanitas, like the one I always visit at the Met, the early seventeenth-century Dutch still life with a skull and a writing quill, an expired lamp with its wisp of smoke—these objects of the writer scattered around, all in vain. The film makes me uncomfortable, Shirley Clarke asking Jason Holliday behind the scenes, "What else you got? What makes you cry?" as he gets more and more inebriated, his life story compelled from him. John tells me about all the regulars who contact him at the museum down the street, where he works as a librarian. People from all over the country, who have vast research questions that often lead nowhere, sometimes various conspiracy theories. John tells me he worries that, when he is making connections in his own writing and thinking, he is like the people calling his library, seeing connections that aren't there. But that's all I do lately too—I try to follow connections.

I realize, looking at my notes now, that this building has been closed for some time, although I haven't returned to Midtown in over a year.

It took Rilke a year to filter through the shocks of the city, to begin to transmogrify the experience of arriving in Paris into language. In a long letter, penned on July 18, 1903, to Lou Andreas-Salomé, a year after he first arrived, he begins to become the other self of his fictional journals. Remembering this recent past, he writes of a porousness to the suffering of others, these people with their melancholy gazes thrust out into the streets, in crowds, for where they sleep he does not know, how he feels wrenched into their lives. In this unreal landscape, time has become layered and confused. This great fear has taken him back to military school, where he felt completely alone, a boy among boys, and now in the city he is alone again, the carts drive right over him as if he doesn't exist. This fear has been growing for some time, taking the quiet green out of his rural retreat with his wife and child, and growing as huge as a house or street or city while in Paris. At night he reads Baudelaire and feels dazed by this companionship, and by his new experiences with poverty. When writing of these street figures, these fragments of caryatids, as if the city is a ruin, Rilke is also thinking constantly through the figures of the sculptor, whose monograph he is supposed to be writing. His eyes are hurting, his hands too, he writes Clara upon arriving at the sculptor's run-down estate in the suburbs, the outside pavilion of dazzling white plaster figures, these gigantic showcases filled with fragments. A piece of arm and leg and body is for Rodin an entire thing, he writes his wife, who probably knew this, as she herself had apprenticed with the sculptor. Nothing is lacking. He describes to her tables, model stands, chests of drawers, all covered with little figures of baked clay, the sculptor's miniature body fragments, or *abattis*. These cases resemble a medical museum, like the small, crammed, harshly lit room of small wax figures the sculptor would frequent in the later nineteenth century at the Hôtel-Dieu. Some speculate that Rodin later visited hospitals, a ball of clay in his pocket. Hand surgeons can now identify the various neurological problems present in his models of convulsive hands. Like the blessing left hand, whose original model  appears to have a form of Dupuytren's contracture, the condition named for Guillaume Dupuytren, the chief surgeon at the Hôtel-Dieu, who pioneered the corrective procedure, and was best known for treating Napoleon Bonaparte's hemorrhoids. There is something anatomical to Rilke's gaze in these descriptions of his initial encounters with the Paris public, the palsied figures and gestures he describes, like the hands of working-class men the sculptor observed from life. The oddly clasped hands of the begging crone that paralyzes the neurasthenic young nobleman in the novel, who watches the pencil emerging slowly from those open hands, and realizes he is supposed to buy it. The lengthy passage in the letter following a man suffering from St. Vitus's dance—a convulsive energy to the writing, as if the poet is performing this man's convulsions down the street on the page, which he saves in its entirety for the novel. Walking down the boulevard St. Michel to the Bibliothèque nationale, he witnesses the crowd's collective gaze at a slender man, who keeps grabbing his black overcoat collar, folding it back down with both hands, hopping, as if pretending to trip or stumble. He begins to follow him, witnessing his jerking and twitching. The disquiet moving through his body. He notices how the man struggles for control, attempts to appear casual and composed. He dances on the bridge, a crowd circling around him. Rilke doesn't go to the library that day. He writes, What book could have been strong enough to help me get past what was inside me?

Perhaps, Bhanu writes me, to begin *Drifts* I have to find a *door*. As I receive her email that fall, a compassionate answer to my feelings of block with this ongoing project, I was meditating upon a large book—still open on my desk now—featuring reproductions of Albrecht Dürer's engravings *Melencolia I* and *Saint Jerome in His Study*. For some time, I had been hoping to write about these images. When Bhanu wrote me this, I felt it was no coincidence that Dürer derives from a word for "door." All that fall I was infected by the drawings and prints of the Renaissance son of a Nuremberg metalworker. I have been thinking of this diptych as Dürer's meditation on the space of thought. Often I have stared at the facing pages, measuring the clutter and chaos of *Melencolia I*, on the left, with the order and clarity of the scholar on the right, his well-lit and industrious *studioli* with his content and sleepy animals at his feet. How cluttered the scene on the left, the space conjured there—it feels like my mind now. The angel of melancholy is surrounded by tools of mathematics and precision: a sphere, a lamp, a measuring instrument, a cutting tool (a scythe perhaps), some wood, a numbered chart, an hourglass, a hammer, a bell, other tools. The angel has keys around her waist, the *putto*, or blind baby cherub, is writing in the open notebook on his lap. The scales hanging from a wall, a big rhomboid structure in the background, a landscape in the distance, a rainbow, underneath a funny flying rat carrying the sign that reads MELENCOLIA I. The angel's expression is furrowed, her hand on her cheek, her body hunched over, the posture a mood. The hourglass represents the urgencies of time.

I think of how Dürer was in his early forties when he made *Melencolia I*. The same year, he completed the charcoal drawing of his elderly mother, *Portrait of the Artist's Mother at the Age of 63*, which he worked on when she was dying. His mother who bore eighteen children. He records the ravages of her face. After his youth, he portrayed other aging faces but not his own. His last self-portrait was in 1500, at the age of twenty-eight. His bearded Jesus face, his noble brown coat with the fur collar. John points out to me how the hands are often skewed in early self-portrait drawings, like Dürer's done in a mirror when he was thirteen. Drawing in a mirror required a direct gaze and an active, moving hand (which was difficult to portray). Often the mirror image of the drawing hand is obscured, hidden behind the visible hand's sleeve. Perhaps it's impossible to record the self at the immediate moment of contemplation, John emails me from work. Perhaps, he jokes, the study is really named *Melencolia I,* the "I" as in first person, as opposed to *Melencolia One*.

In the morning, the parade of dogs with their owners. We all cross the street to avoid altercations. This morning Genet growled at a friendly pit bull—I had to pull his thrashing body away, only for him to whimper when the same dog was behind us on the way back. I think of the seemingly identical feral cats that lurk outside of the new cat house and I begin to see the house and the sidewalks as a dimensional space, like one of Dürer's engravings, as if these are all the same striped cat drawn in different poses. I take photographs of the copycats as they laze around on spookily warm days. Walking from Midtown to the Village right before Halloween, the golden retriever with the huge orange lion mane lying glumly on the ground while everyone took its picture.

In November the warm weather continues to be unnerving. "Happy Apocalypse!" I begin greeting people. On my days off I walk around my neighborhood and take photographs of the Halloween decorations that are still up. The impressive decorations on the massive porches of some of the grand Victorian houses. Families of mannequins dressed as zombie brides, buried families, dog and cat skeletons, skulls on the ground, flying skeletons hanging from trees. Sometimes just cobwebs strewn over the bushes, over the front of the houses. Which reminds me of the passage I just read about spiderwebs in Wittgenstein's *Philosophical Investigations*: "Here it is difficult to keep our minds above water, as it were, to see that we stick to matters of everyday thought, and not to get on the wrong track where it seems that we have to describe extreme subtleties, which again we are quite unable to describe with the means at our disposal. We feel as if we had to repair a torn spider's web with our fingers." It is while walking around that I can experience what Cornell in his diaries notes as an "absence of wanderlust nervousness." The itchiness subsides as I take photographs. A batlike decoration strung in a tree looks almost exactly like the flying ratlike thing in *Melencolia I*, which appears again, John and I discover, in one of Dürer's *Passion* images.

That late fall, I go back to reading *The Tanners*. "The next morning the painter unpacked his landscapes from their portfolio and first an entire autumn fell out of it. . . ." The fall leaves make the light yellow as I walk around and think about the painters of yellow: Vermeer, Van Gogh, Hopper. What if a work had a sort of weather? I ask my students. What if it could be shot through with yellow light? How sensitive and melancholy Genet is, looking out the window, like a little prince. The rain tranquilizes him. I catch him gazing at me. The strong, vinegary smell of the fruit from the yellowing gingko tree. Like the ferment of vomit. I read somewhere that only the female gingko tree stinks. We can't keep Genet from gobbling up the yellow flesh balls on the sidewalk. Sometime in November, he starts throwing them up in the middle of the night. I wake up in a patch of his yellow-green vomit. So much feels premonitory that fall. While in the death pose at the end of yoga class, I stare at the speaker, made from a hollowed-out butternut squash, hanging from the ceiling of the studio. I realize it replicates the inexplicable squash hanging from the ceiling in Dürer's *Saint Jerome in His Study*. Later we eat at an Ethiopian restaurant and see a decorative squash hanging from the ceiling. There appears to be a vast referentiality everywhere.

One Saturday in the middle of November my father calls me from the emergency room. The exhaustion and panic in his voice. When he calls, the image open on my desktop is the self-portrait of Dürer as a melancholic, pointing at his enlarged spleen like a Christ figure. In one window I am thinking through that image, while in another I am calling up the search box at the Mayo Clinic's website, entering the words "enlarged spleen fatty liver leaking bile." Is my father's urine the color of cola or dark orange? What does it mean that I was reading about melancholy and the humours while my father was in the ER? That bile is the humour of the melancholic? It means nothing, or: it means everything. That this is the mode of collapse.

All November I walk around, entranced and revulsed by trees in the neighborhood. I take hundreds of close-ups of the trees. The scars, holes, and scales of the bark. Like abstract paintings, stripped and haunting. The bulbous protrusions on these tree bodies, how they look at twilight. My uncle, my father's identical twin—did I think he was like one of these trees at the end? I remember years ago, just after he died, sitting around the kitchen table at the old house with my father and my aunt, the medievalist. My father began talking about the bubonic plague, because he has just read a book on the subject. How the modern stems from a third of civilization being killed off. My aunt moves the conversation to puerperal fever and cradle death. This is when I love them the most, feel the most kinship with them. Untangling death, always at a remove of history. We weren't able to discuss the real death at the table, the chair where my father now sat occupied previously by his twin brother, who lived in that house his entire life with his mother and sister. His bones molded into a hunched-over curve, unable to carry the weight of his bloated tumorous belly, the death that resided in him for months. Like the death everyone has housed inside them, as Rilke writes in *The Notebooks of Malte Laurids Brigge*. How John and

I would sit with my uncle, in the living room in the old house, my uncle in his mother's old rocking chair. We asked him about his time in the navy. I read to him from the sports section, announcing the headlines in humorous voices. He enjoyed the tedium of this, of listening to the baseball news. It became difficult to help him upstairs, into his own bed. I remember—his nosebleed on the sheets, how we had to be careful with his body. And then his coma in the hospital, holding his hand.

In the fall of 1907, at a reading in Vienna, Rilke wears a black velvet cape and reads one of the early scenes from his novel in progress, which takes his alter ego from the city to the ancestral house of his childhood. The noble and immense spectacle of the death of his grandfather, whose body grows larger and larger, taking up the space of the old manor house, until the patriarch insists on being carried from one room to another, like a funeral procession for a still living man. What is a novel but a large ancestral estate, after all—there is history in the walls, one demands to be carried into every room, falling into a paroxysm of melancholy and rage when one room is left abandoned. The dogs linger in the room of the dying man, occupying spaces like something out of Velázquez, dancing among the absent-minded and drowsy things. The tall, lean Russian wolfhounds running around the armchairs, reared like heraldic animals, resting their paws on the white-and-gold window sill, the glove-yellow dachshunds on the silk-upholstered easy chair near the window, the sullen setter rubbing against the edge of a table, causing porcelain cups on painted trays to tremble. After reading out loud from this dense and decorative passage, Rilke suffers a nosebleed—

one wonders if it was a precursor of the death he had within him, as his character theorizes that everyone has a death within them, living dormant for two more decades, a cancer of the blood, catalyzed by the prick of one of his favorite roses, while living in Switzerland.

That fall I rely on animal videos to get by, unable to bear the spectacular violence reported in the media, the seemingly constant shootings, dashboard videos of murders of teenagers by police. Instead I watch video of the new baby red pandas at the Prospect Park Zoo, listed as vulnerable because of the deforestation in their native habitat of the Eastern Himalayas. Even with the melancholy of watching animals in captivity, and the intense sadness thinking about the imminent destruction of their species, there is still something soothing about these zoo videos—the slow, silent ambling of these burnished-color baby animals, through grass, climbing on trees, staring at the camera. In counterpoint to these slow, silent videos, the recently circulated video juxtaposing yellow cabs, Times Square, a Gap in Herald Square, as sites of future attack. I walk through the guards armed with assault rifles at Grand Central on the way to and from the Metro-North, thinking of the paranoiac and vulnerable psychic energy of these massive public spaces. I smile at the large dogs, who are serious, working. The feelings of a strained fellowship amidst waves of people, waiting to trudge upstairs.

John and I muse that Dürer really originated some version of the soothing animal video. All fall I think about the animals in the margins of Dürer's prints. The old skinny dog curled up in *Melencolia I* versus the contented sleeping dog and lion in *Saint Jerome*, their paws almost touching. My own dog is aloof and melancholic in the other room, he needs his own space in the mornings, although at some point he will decide to curl up on the little rug underneath my desk. Throughout the day, from the Met print room where John is doing research, he texts me images of the tiny affenpinscher with the lion-cut who reoccurs in the margins of Dürer's *Passion* scenes, striking sassy poses in scenes of Christ's torture. Later I read that Dürer laid a painting of himself out in the sun to dry, and the self-portrait was so realistic his dog licked the face of the painting. (John: How do we know this? Did it leave a mark?) But, as he writes me, this suggests for us two important things: (a) Dürer had a dog and (b) Dürer allowed his dog to lick his face. I like the idea that the Dürer who was wrecked with this crushing project, these scenes of death, who considered the Passion of Christ the greatest artistic subject, also put his little dog there to make him happy. The beautiful shape Genet is making now, a curve at rest. His yawn and stretch. His darling little mongrel face, perhaps part affenpinscher, we don't know. His little gray goatee. I have taken to calling him "The Bearded One," after Dürer's nickname. Genet, my little panther I study. He stares at me with glowing amber eyes.

The intense pleasure I take from my dogwalker's updates. She tells me which dogs, from his neighborhood pack of bearded wizards, he has walked with that day. Most are duos with names that make me happy: Betty White and Sonic, Fonzie and Annabelle. I'm glad Genet has friends, because he is not good at meeting new dogs, because of his fear aggression. He's not friendly, I have to tell people when we are out walking. Though he is silent and worried when others bark at him, usually tiny furry dogs more neurotic than him. During the day I watch my dog, his melancholy and sensitivity, his aloofness yet desire for affection, and I think that we get the animals that we deserve. As I wait for my bagel, I watch the outside table where the dog and baby people congregate. I have to stand off to the side with Genet so he doesn't freak out at dogs passing by. I watch the woman who is my neighborhood nemesis, with her Pomeranian on her lap—now dressed in the same identical brown sweater with skull and crossbones that Genet has, which cannot, I think, be a coincidence. She is my nemesis because she lets her little dog off the leash in the neighborhood, as she meanders slowly behind him, and also because once, when her little dog ran up to Genet and I scooped him up, she said something in Polish to me with a tone that I interpreted to mean, What's wrong with unfriendly people like you, with your unfriendly dogs? As I'm watching them now, she lets her dog under the communal table, where it takes a little shit, which she then scoops up with a napkin and ambles over to the garbage can to throw out.

By the end of the semester, I am so stuffed full with the words of others that I have just enough energy to scribble down notes of my own, hoping to remember them later. My favorite student, the cinephile, confesses to me that his depression has returned. I remember, at that meeting at the beginning of the semester, the lawyer telling us that the students' depression is not our problem. I worry over them, the ones who drop out. I write letters to their advisers, full-time tenured professors, who often don't reply. There is a student from the Midwest, a scholarship kid, who has not shown up most of the semester. When she comes to class it's obvious she hasn't slept all night, her head on the table, and when I call on her she is all hollowed eyes and irritation. She picks apart everyone else's writing and is sensitive about her own. When we meet, I try to push, and she bristles at me. She likes to list the writers that she loves, lyric essayists she wants to write like, although, she notes, she also wants to make money writing. Didn't you write, like, one of those "girl" novels, she said to me at one of our early meetings. I can tell when she says this she's trying to irritate me, and it works. I think she reminds me too much of myself, the bad student I used to be, like a ghost with chaotic energy. Danielle writes me that she had to learn boundaries with students—I have to save something for myself, she says. And yet I wonder sometimes if my career is not in writing but in depression.

Leaving the train station, returning home, I hear the bleatings of the broken mechanical horse outside the Tibetan restaurant. Originally it played "Yankee Doodle Dandy," but it has become increasingly demented, making erratic and glitchy sounds. Eating my lunch, the pale blue eggs trickled out a blue pus at my desk, while I was meeting with a student. How repulsed my students probably are by the pungent salads I bring from home. Back at the apartment, I feed Genet and eat a piece of chocolate while standing up. When I take him outside, he walks briskly in the dark. He is always spooked walking at twilight. It was twilight when he was attacked by a large dog off its leash, where we last lived, in North Carolina. Halloween decorations are still up—a fogged window, the words HELP ME scrawled on the window from inside, where a standing figure appears to have its hands against the frosted glass. An orange hand sticking up from the ground. I remember, now, writing this, that it was around Halloween when he was attacked as well. How we stumbled into the house of the two men watching from a nearby porch, watched as the dog dragged the puppy into the street thrashing him back and forth—worried him in his mouth—that's the word for it, "worried." I look this up later and it's from the Old English *wyrgan*, to strangle, changed gradually to mean to cause anxiety. A dog's pleasure at clamping

down with his incisors, like Genet with his bone or
stuffed animal or this large dog with my puppy in his
mouth. My puppy's yelps of distress, as I threw myself
onto them, into the street. We could have been hit by
a passing car. He was a doctor, the man said, although
Genet backed away from him, too nervous and shaking to be examined, his tiny puncture wounds covered
by bloodied matted hair. I can see now, just behind my
cowering puppy, a bowl of Halloween candy still out in
their deluxe kitchen with its marble island and counter-
tops. The art on the walls. One of them drove us the
few blocks home, me cradling Genet, both of us shaking. Out walking now in our neighborhood the trees
look like sculptures in the night. One house bright with
Christmas lights for a night shoot. The camera crews
appear often around here. Several television shows film
in the neighborhood, which can stand for any city suburb. I think this one is for *The Americans*, the show about
Soviet spies living in the DC suburbs in the Reagan era.
It's a show where almost everyone turns out to be a spy.
There's a surreality to entering one place masquerading
as another, the present masquerading as another time.
When I first moved here *Boardwalk Empire* was filming, and in the middle of summer there was fake snow
on the vintage cars. Later in the summer there were
Greek letters on one of the houses and red cups litter-
ing the lawn, one of the grand Victorians remade as a
University of Iowa fraternity house on *Girls*.

In November my editor quits the publishing company where I am contracted to turn in *Drifts* at the end of the summer. I panic. I don't know now whether I will write a book, as this seems like another reason not to write it. To have one's future work contracted by a corporation seems at odds with my desire to write a nervous and diaristic text. The desire to quit is so intense for me now. How confusing, how it competes inside me with this still ravishing desire to be writing a book that never has to be completed. This is when Sofia and I begin writing each other in earnest. Off social media, and in despair over our manuscripts. I had first interacted with Sofia when she commented on my blog years ago, back when I kept a blog, and we kept in touch sporadically, sending each other lists of our readings. After I bought *Antwerp*, it didn't surprise me at all to learn that she was reading it at the same time. On my desk is a Portuguese edition of "Bartleby, the Scrivener" that one of John's researchers gave to him at the library, bound on both ends, so you have to destroy it to open it. I keep on meaning to send it to her. I write to Sofia, I think I cling so much to Bartleby because it is a story of antagonism toward professionalism and toward New York—it is the New York *no*, the refusal of concepts of success and industriousness, of participation. And also because Bartleby refuses to tell anything about himself, which is a longing for me. Herman Melville wrote "Bartleby" after the failure of his most recent book, dismissed in the press, and so it is a portrait of a writer as well. I feel myself shrinking, I write to Sofia, who diagnoses my choking feeling as a nervous condition. I write to her, I feel instead of publishing as if I am slowly decreating, like a calm Chicken Little. The other day I tried to write the word "digressions" and wrote instead "depressions," and I wonder if this is the form I've been searching for: a "depression," a kind of digression, sinking deeper and deeper.

Lately I have been fixing my students' writing problems in my sleep. Former students write me, wanting to meet, wanting advice, letters of recommendation, solace. Everyone wants to be a writer, but they want to be successful writers, famous writers, and I don't know how to advise with that. Writing is a life of constant rejection. It never stops, the rejection. My friends who write me looking for help with their publishing woes. I realize I've been trying to fix everyone's existential crises except my own. Which I then pour forth in letters, in a new genre I've been thinking of as the *complaint*. I worry, when I do not hear from Sofia or Anna or others, that I have said too much, that I have annoyed them. Yet sometimes I'm the one who drops the conversation. It can become too much, to be in conversation. I am reminded of those lines from *The Tanners*, "Writing a letter, you get carried away and make incautious remarks. In letters, the soul always wishes to do the talking and generally it makes a fool of itself. So it's best I don't write." To have countless correspondents, to crave that communion, and yet to be removed, to need privacy. Cornell copying down into his journal a line from a Rilke biography: "In the letters written between 1910 and 1914 we find Rilke (continually) expressing a longing for human companionship and affection, and then, often immediately afterwards asking whether he could really respond to such companionship if it were offered to him, and wondering whether, after all, his real task might not lie elsewhere." I write to Sofia of my longing to be a nobody. Is it possible, still, to leave one's name, one's face, to transcend oneself in the work? Sofia writes me of these panic attacks she has lately where she worries it's gone, that she's lost it, perhaps, she writes me, it's like your choking. For I will never again have the solitude of being totally unknown, a zero, creating in that freedom, she writes. I tell her of an epigraph to a book I plan to write, Foucault noting that he writes in order not to have a face, and she says she knows it well, it is actually the epigraph to a book she plans to write, the narrator a zero, dissolved, not like the books she is currently working on, steeped in identity and community. I've ceased marveling at what Sofia calls our *parallel utopian concepts of literature*. She writes me that today her son played soccer, and every time her son's team scored, a kid on the losing team would encourage his own team by piping in "It's still zero-zero!" It reminded me of the state I have to psych myself into in order to write anything. I have to pretend I've never failed, she writes, that I'm still at the beginning, that everything is still zero-zero. This effort of will to imagine you're still at the beginning and everything is still possible, even though you know where you really are. It's still zero-zero, Kate. It's always zero-zero.

On a Sunday in November, to distract ourselves from
thinking about the crisis of my father's illness, John and
I take several trains to the Lenox Hill neighborhood
on the Upper East Side—a penthouse apartment that
housed a very small portion of the vast art collection of
the spouse of a major Venezuelan media mogul, responsible for donating a major collection of Latin American
geometric abstraction to the MoMA—to look at an in-
formal display of colonialist travel books from Alexander
von Humboldt, the nineteenth-century naturalist and
explorer of Latin America. The display was accompa-
nied by these exotifying landscape print portfolios. It
was a kind of cocktail party that we'd never normally
attend, or be invited to, a very New York and seemingly
humorless mixture of culture workers and moneyed col-
lectors, but John had been asked to go by a colleague to
represent the library. It was an apartment where no one
seemed to live, but occasionally assistants would inhabit
to rearrange and store the art. The entire time we were
looking at the books, laid out on a dining table like a
banquet, John kept on whispering in my ear that he felt
he was in César Aira's *An Episode in the Life of a Landscape Painter*, the speculative work about the nineteenth-
century German artist Johann Moritz Rugendas, who

mentored under Humboldt, who while traveling into the Pampas in Argentina is attacked by various calamities, including being hit by lightning while riding his horse and becoming horrifically disfigured, his vision altered, until the novella itself takes on the feel of a hallucinogenic landscape painting. The only thing I was interested in was a book previously owned by the art collector's grandfather, a media mogul who was also an ornithologist at the American Museum of Natural History in the 1930s. The book featured gorgeous, outlandishly hand-painted Colombian pigeons. Since I had just been thinking of Joseph Cornell, his fascination with pigeons, his Natural Museum boxes, it felt like a connection I couldn't explain. What does it mean, I wrote Sofia, that John and I felt we were in a César Aira novel? Afterward we walked around the early Netherlandish room at the Met. My favorite painting in that room, which I return to often, is *Portrait of a Woman*—I love how distracted the woman looks, her jeweled fingers woven through her prayer book. I am also always compelled by the lactating Virgins, their pointed, naked breasts. On the train home seeing pairs of pale people who looked like twins, almost as if they were out of a Netherlandish painting, with their translucent skin, but in contemporary dress, with shopping bags and running shoes.

Sometime that month, I see the old woman crossing the street. Slung on her arm a black Coach purse, with its familiar gold clasp. It is a purse I recognize intimately, as it is identical to the one that I use when I take the old camera out on my walks, as I did all that fall. I was startled to see that purse on her, as it was the same exact purse my mother used to carry, the purse I would bring to the hospital for her when she wasn't herself anymore, that she would guard as some memory of her former identity.

Outside on the porch, with a coat on so Genet can sit in the sun. He's still vomiting up the yellow gingko balls at night. Yesterday I didn't leave the house. I lounged around, and bled, and watched TV on my computer, and laid books on top of me, in the hope that I would read them. The day before, I had participated in a faculty reading that, up until the hour before, I was sure I was going to cancel. I told myself that if I had to do this reading I would write new work for this event, which I've known about for months. I wanted to write about Dürer's *Melencolia I,* but instead I continued my practice of filling up my notebooks with notes and little fragments. So I read a section on Victorian postmortem photography from the book on my mother, which I still can't find anyone willing to publish in its current form. It felt alienating reading from a book I had already written, about another period in my life, even though it hadn't yet been published. It was as if that book was from another self, as if the writing of the book allowed me to become another self while moving through it. What would it be like, I wondered, thinking of the genius grant winner, to write a self in the time you were the self you wrote about in your book, so you were sure it was you? At the reading, I was followed by a graphic novelist who documented the nervous condition of being thirty-seven—my same age—in a witty way, a *creamy way*, Bhanu wrote to me yesterday, after I wrote her in distress, which I realize now is often when I write to her. To conclude the reading, one of the full-time professors, a much-awarded poet, read a cycle of history poems for more than forty minutes, even though we were told to read for no more than ten. Since I was in the front row, I had to try to keep an alert expression on my face, although I was falling asleep. At the dinner afterward, the head of creative writing, seated to my left, remarked to me that the graphic novelist gave the best reading, and, smiling, I agreed, although quickly she realized who she was talking to and apologized. It was true, anyway, I hadn't given a good reading. Only polite clapping afterward. A donor was apparently seated to the right of me at the dinner, and the department head, a medieval scholar, whispered to me to try to be charming, and only later did I have time to reflect how odd it was for her to ask me to perform that role. But this is what I do, usually, smile and agree. This is why, I believe, Walser is so important to me, his passivity and servility that's undercut with pricklier energy, when he sits down and writes. Writing is a way to counter that other, public, self, who must be constantly polite in order not to get fired, in this exhausting life as what I've begun to think of as the amazing traveling adjunct. When the professor interviewed me for the class, she told me she didn't have time to read my books, which she gestured to, a little pile of two on her desk. I felt so depleted the entire

evening—it didn't help that I had bled through my trousers, on the train there, so I was also worried more than
anything that I would get blood on the new white silk
blouse that I'd purchased that month, in anticipation
of the reading, which was ridiculous and unnecessary,
but often how I psych myself up to do public events. I
spent the entire day in bed, dreading the reading, and
the entire next day recovering from it. I wrote to Bhanu,
Perhaps this shame and self-loathing is partially why I
am a writer. Perhaps because of the feeling of invisibility I felt as a child. I didn't know artists or intellectuals
or even women with professional careers growing up in
the lower-middle-class Midwestern suburbs. How star-
tling this was for me, when I began teaching at these
schools, these students were children of doctors and
lawyers and professors and artists, they had gone to special schools for the arts or boarding schools, they knew
they were brilliant, they wanted to be successes, they
wanted their families to recognize them, and their families did recognize them. This initially filled me with
bitterness, although I've since gotten over it and can
regard it with some distance. Because I had arrived too
early for the reading, I had wandered around the dance
department. Spying a poster of Yvonne Rainer, I wondered briefly if maybe I could have been a modern dance
major—the fantasy that my parents would have allowed
such a thing. Would I then have been more happy, more
well-adjusted, more confident? At the dinner: the department head, two other full-time professors—one a
fairly known novelist a decade or so older than me, and

the other a much older, celebrated novelist, the grande dame of the small creative writing department—as well as the graphic novelist my age, who was also a visiting professor with one class. The full-timers complained about their students, their need for trigger warnings especially. I found myself siding entirely with my students, how I had learned from this generation, how they thought of consent in different ways than I did when I was their age. The atmosphere became intense, perhaps hostile toward me, this unknown usurper. I remember now, the full-timers insisted on giving me money for a cab ride home after the dinner, because it was late and would take me more than an hour to get home. I refused politely but finally took the fifty dollars they pooled, which only cemented for me their perception of my relative youthfulness and their awareness of my precarity.

Earlier that day, before the reading, I had left the house
only to pick up my white silk blouse from the dry cleaner's. I chat there often with the perennially disquieted
Vera, who over these three years I have convinced to
like me—she sometimes smiles at me when I walk by,
and I wave at her, and she waves back, a victory. When
I moved here, I took in to the corner dry cleaner's a
kimono-like navy jacket that had a slim navy sash of
the same material. When I wore the jacket afterward,
I became increasingly aware that the navy sash felt of a
different material, even though it was the identical color
and length of my sash. I took it back to Vera, repeatedly,
showing her the sash, both of us exasperated, and she
would show me the spare or lost belts and sashes they
kept, clipped to a hanging belt, none of which matched.
Finally, a month later, Vera told me she had found my
sash, which matched the thicker, sturdier material of the
jacket, as opposed to the silkier sash she'd given me. I
had thought I was going crazy. That subtle feeling—
something is amiss, although everything appears normal on the surface. It has stayed with me the entire time
I've been in this city. Vera is perpetually at war with
the owner, Mr. Kim. In the summer, Mr. Kim refuses
to put on the air-conditioning, and Vera complains of

the heat. But the real issue is the question of time. Mr. Kim often tells customers their clothes will be done far earlier than Vera would like, because it's just the two of them working there. Vera is often so dyspeptic when I see her, so I let her complain to me for a while—which makes me happy, to offer this service. On this visit, a man in front of me was angry that she couldn't find an item he'd dropped off months ago. When he left I asked her whether this happens often, customers losing their patience with her, over items they should have picked up long before. She told me the story of a woman who last week tried to pick up her wedding dress, which she dropped off three years earlier. The woman was incensed that the dress looked dingy, and tried to insist she shouldn't have to pay for it, which, as Vera explained to her and to me, of course it did, it spent three years encased in plastic at a humid dry cleaner's. I listened to the story and made the appropriate noises in response. Vera is also the name of my deceased grandmother, and even though this Vera speaks Spanish and has thin blond hair she pulls back into a ponytail, and is only in her early fifties, I think, she reminds me of my grandmother, with her fleshy brown arms fanning herself in the humidity, and also my grandmother's vitality and temper. My grandmother half-paralyzed in a wheelchair, still perched like a queen over the plastic-coated kitchen table, ruling over everyone with a grabber, dictating control over her two adult children she lived with, like Joseph Cornell's tyrannical mother who he loved so dearly. My grandmother for decades worked linens at Marshall Field's, and we would visit her there when we were children. The way Vera smooths her tan hand over the plastic casing reminds me of watching my grandmother, with her brown wrinkled hands and yellow nails, expertly fold and smooth a fitted sheet. Genet is in the other room on the bed as I'm writing this. He is curled up on my pillow, near a small spot of dried blood on the sheets. He has licked the spot and it has grown wet and wider and faded. I curl around him and smell him, kissing the white diamond on his little barrel chest. I feel the most voluptuous when it's just me and my dog alone like this, in an unmade bed, when I can bury my head into his neck, weeping.

Could this work, could *Drifts*, unfold like a dream? It
is still yellow outside but the trees are now bare. I bring
The Tanners with me to the local café, along with Renee
Gladman's *Event Factory*, another yellow book. On the
first page of *Event Factory*: "The city was large, yellow,
and tender." On a gloomy, rainy day, I take photographs
of the wet cats in the alley. In early December I write to
my TV correspondent in Idaho that I'm feeling both miserable and joyful, blocked and slow, yet porous and sensitive. He has just learned he is becoming a parent. He's
now making lists of writers with kids, to try to bolster himself. Elizabeth Hardwick, for instance. Clarice Lispector.
Susan Sontag. Later, however, there's something I want to
say to him about this list he was making, but I don't say
anything.

I keep getting consumed by the constant tragedies,
passively participating in this collective mourning online. Then I binge-watch crime procedurals (the fantasy
perhaps of a functional justice system), so as to avoid a
constant intake of news. An ambient political depression.
The pulsing vulnerabilities of my students, as they too
deal with all of this. How they attempt to write through
their traumas. How I don't often know how to help them

hold space for this trauma, but I wish to, and by the end
of the semester I feel like an exhausted social worker.
I'm starting to feel run-down, to get swollen glands. At
the close of the semester I felt sure that what I needed to
feel better, to be a new person, was a new red lipstick—
an expensive red, housed in a silver or gold case. I scroll
through my phone on the train home, fixated by the
slight derivations of shades of red. I go to the Sephora
off Union Square after Monday's class. The park is filled
with homeless animals, the dogs, the litter of kittens living on a woman like she is their house, but I look away.
That feeling still in the pit of my stomach. At the Sephora
I buy a red Dolce & Gabbana lipstick, which I've decided
on after lengthy research, but it is too orange. The next
day I return the lipstick at a different Sephora off Times
Square, and get a YSL red, which I don't like either but
don't bother returning. The patient and bored salespeople
who stand and watch as I present to them my screaming
red mouth. The red stains on my teeth, my fingers. What
I probably want is a new face and new personality. To be
someone other than myself.

Didn't Sontag, like, have a Sephora VIP card, one of
my students in my seminar asks. We are discussing her
writing on photography. There had recently been a news
item—her email archive had been made public. Let her
shop in private! I snap back, and they are surprised by my
sudden vehemence.

The little dog by my side is beginning to resemble the doll-like bearded lynx in that Dürer sketch *Sketches of Animals and Landscapes*, which is the title for the section of *Drifts* I am transcribing from my notes. The silver-blue fur and peach-pink flesh of the baboon, the only colored element in the drawing. The sleepy lions. The two stacked views of the same bridge in a landscape from different perspectives. Genet brings me his red large geometric ball. I don't notice him now, too immersed in my process of transcription, so he goes looking for another toy to entice me to play. He now pushes his rubber bone into my hand. Writing this, I am reminded of the beginning of *Austerlitz*, where Sebald remembers wandering into a zoo in Antwerp, and links the intent gaze of the nocturnal animals to the gazes of philosophers and writers, illustrating the passage with the eyes of an unidentified Wittgenstein. An opening that strangely dissolves into a visual memory of a crowd of travelers at the grand train station.

I love reading about Cornell's epistolary friendship with Marianne Moore—both of them living with their claustrophobic mothers, her in Brooklyn, him in Queens, the caretaker/nurses of their families. They wrote each other of rare books and animals. How he writes her of the referential library of his mind:

> *Dear Miss Moore,*
> *For some time I have been trying to feel collected*
> *enough to write to you about an interesting thought*
> *or two that has come to me in the past year or so. But*
> *there seems to be such a complexity, a sort of endless*
> *cross-indexing of detail (intoxicatingly rich) in*
> *connection with what and how I feel that I never seem*
> *to come to the point of doing anything about it.*

The other day I made my way to the office and looked at the book that's been open on my desk for two years now. In a quick spirit of collage, I had placed a postcard of a photograph of Joseph Cornell against Dürer's *Melencolia I* while attempting to wrestle with this seemingly intractable pile of notes. The photograph is of Cornell as an old man, sitting in a hard chair against a background of

faded paisley wallpaper, his hand resting a book against
his head, eyes closed, as if he is mimicking the posture
of Dürer's angel. In the foreground, overflowing shelves
of files and boxes. I read somewhere, in a book about
Cornell, that *horror vacui*, fear of empty spaces, was a
specifically Victorian malady. Is this our real phobia with
our books? I write to Sofia. The horror—and perversely
the desire—to be empty?

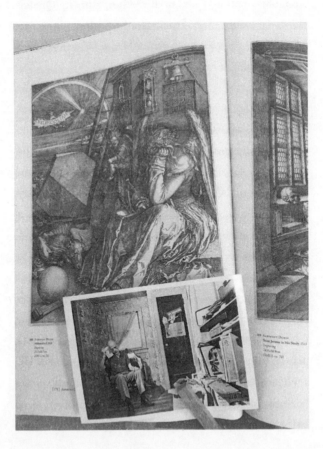

At times in the morning, I feel my office, with my little dog asleep curled up on the rug, is the calm space of Saint Jerome's study, especially when I have arranged and stacked all the notes and scraps on my desk, or hidden them off to the side. I am reminded of a discovery of this period of reading, that the local hermit saint of Nuremberg, where Dürer was born and lived, was Saint Sebaldus, his relics enshrined in the church Dürer and his family attended. My dog, contemplative on the carpet, catches me looking at him and jumps up to the chair. So distracted by my father's health, I often can only scribble down notes. The last time I spoke to my father, he told me that he's waiting a month to go to a liver specialist. It frustrates me, this refusal to deal with his body, with the possibility that he might have his twin's liver cancer. I know he doesn't want to know. His voice sounds exhausted. I ask him how much he slept the night before. I can imagine him sitting up in his chair, in pain. It is the fact of my father's solitude that afflicts me. Genet lies on the little shag rug under the desk. He wants me to pick him up and cuddle him, and I do.

Yesterday I watched *Tokyo Story* on my computer. The pathos of elderly parents who travel to Tokyo to see their adult children, who are too busy to spend time with them. To watch these characters inhabit homely interiors, the mother and father slowly folding items in and out of a small leather carrier. The grief and ongoingness of the everyday. And the magnificent, tender face of Setsuko Hara, who plays the dutiful daughter-in-law and widow. It had just been reported that she died earlier in the fall, at the age of ninety-five. She never married, living a life of seclusion, refusing all interviews and photographs. That moment at the end of the film, between her and the youngest daughter— "Isn't life disappointing?" "I think so." An ecstasy almost to her look of resignation, so open and pained in its cheerfulness. At some point watching the film I began to weep and couldn't stop. I am still shaken by the experience of watching it. Thinking of my widowed father up all night, folding laundry, watching movies. He tells me he is having trouble reading his book on the history of punctuation. My little dog's chin is on my notebook, he sighs heavily into the desk as I scratch his little beard. I know now I must go visit him, as soon as the semester is over, even though I dread it.

The last two weeks of December, I am sick in bed with a respiratory infection. I flip through books, a biography of Wittgenstein's family I began on the plane ride home from Chicago, having flown in to take my father to specialists, his illness still a mystery. How regressive I get after I see my father. I am no longer a writer, someone who thinks. I am a complete nobody. Two weeks ago *Drifts* felt possible, and now I feel time escaping me, and me allowing it to escape. On Christmas Day I force myself out of bed to go on a walk. It was in the seventies that weekend—it felt suspicious not to need a hat or coat. In that widely circulated photograph of Robert Walser dead in the snow on Christmas Day, I find the most touching detail to be his hat, some paces away, thrown by the velocity of his fall or the wind.

When I look through my winter photographic studies from that period, the lighting is cooler, grayer. The trees change, look starker, more sculptural. The decaying brown leaves at the end, stripped trees, the howling white birch. Besides trees, stone lions, and houses, which remain unmoving except for sudden attacks of weather, I've been making a series of photos of pieces of colored fabric in the landscape. A shock of color out of nowhere.

The bright orange monk robes in the distance. The vivid blue of a T-shirt on the ground, today, a purple broken umbrella amidst the grass and browning leaves, a baby's bib with LOVE repeated in rainbow letters in a bush. Roses in the winter, growing in concrete gardens. I take several photographs of a card made of gold foil on the sidewalk. It connected to a passage I read today in Enrique Vila-Matas's *Bartleby & Co*: "Walser wanted to be a walking nobody, and the vanity he loved was like that of Fernando Pessoa, who once, on throwing a chocolate silver-foil wrapper to the ground, said that, in doing so, he had thrown away life." I wonder if I'm suffering from the paralysis that Vila-Matas describes, this "Bartleby's syndrome." But the longing to write is stronger than ever, as is my constant notetaking.

I crop the photograph taken in the fall of the old woman outside in her garden, pulling weeds. The crouch of the photo. Its slowness. The coloration burnt and somber. The nakedness of her lawn.

Vila-Matas on Robert Walser: "But the vanity he loved had nothing to do with the drive for personal success, rather it was the sort that is a tender display of what is minimal, what is fleeting."

To put everything I love into my boxes, the small and the tender.

Right before the New Year, a long walk around the
neighborhood in the winter light with my camera. A
man stops his car to ask me why I'm taking pictures of
the houses. I'm taking pictures of the trees, not the houses, I say to him. Although I am also taking photographs
of the houses, the decaying and crumbling exteriors of
the many abandoned and run-down houses, their rotted
doors and windows. I've thought of doing that myself,
someday, he says, and, rolling up his window, drives
off. I puzzled over this the rest of the walk home, as I
stopped to take detailed photographs of the patterns of
the trees. People always say that about art, or any form
of keeping time, of collecting. That they could do it—
but of course they could do it, the thing is, whether they
do or not. There is one particular tree, a white birch,
that I continually take photographs of, its circling patterns that look like Munch's scream. In some ways I
know I am taking the same photograph, or some version of the same photograph, and there's almost no dis-
cernible difference between the hole I focused on a few
weeks ago and the same one today, except perhaps light
and season. I am now wearing a long coat and leather
gloves, although it is still unseasonably warm outside.
Velvety green moss grows in one of the recesses that

I focused on today, and perhaps that is new, or maybe I was just able to see it differently today. Trees register the changing of time almost imperceptibly. I think of the sequoias sequence in Hitchcock's *Vertigo*. Jimmy Stewart takes Kim Novak as Madeleine to Muir Woods, trying to get her to remember if she's ever been there before. When he tells her that some of the trees are two thousand years old, she remarks that trees are the oldest living things. "I don't like it," she says, "knowing I have to die." They walk over to the cross-section of a tree cut down, its rings mapping across centuries. The music becomes ominous. Kim Novak, now playing Madeleine haunted by the spirit of Carlotta, places her gloved finger on the tree, whispering to it: "Somewhere here I was born. There I died. It was only a moment for you; you took no notice." Her coil of silver-blond hair a spiral of infinity. She walks off, as if sleepwalking, ghostlike in her silvery coat. I am struck by the sublimity of the massive trees as I move about, I feel small when I also place my hand on a knot on the tree and look up, a gesture I am more likely to do on a solitary walk, but John tells me I still do this when walking together. When I was a child, my father often took us to the local arboretum. Still every time I go on a walk or to a botanical garden with him—it's been some time since he was well enough to walk long distances—he has a habit that John and I often mimic, lovingly, of stopping at the foot of one of the massive trees, reading the marker, and then repeating the name of the tree in an exaggerated, loud cadence: "Loblolly pine. Okay." Here in my neighborhood there are little placards on some, pointing out their species. Tulip tree or various pines. I read somewhere that Wittgenstein, too, liked to identify trees on his long walks. That story of Wittgenstein sitting with a fellow philosopher in the garden, pointing at a tree and saying over and over, "I know that is a tree." When a stranger enters the garden, Wittgenstein tells them, "We are not insane, we are doing philosophy." I know this is a tree . . . I wanted to take photographs of the two dying trees outside of my father's house, with decaying limbs, one of them sprouting giant mushrooms. These early memories I have of being alone and playing, and whispering to the two massive trees in the front yard of my childhood home, watching and listening as they rustled in the wind, and feeling I had done something to effect that movement. If I had gone outside to take photographs, I knew my father wouldn't have understood. It felt impossible to try to explain to him how unbearably beautiful I found the decay of these trees from my childhood. And that art for me is a way to remark upon solitude, for myself and others. A way to mark time.

As I look through the photographs, I am still moved by the solemnity of the growths and textures on the trees, the hauntingness of the holes, like abstract paintings. To be afraid of holes—or not a phobia, really, to be intensely drawn to them—it is becoming clear to me that the narrative I am interested in deals more with holes than what is filled in. I don't need to remember what the trees looked like, but how moved I felt when

I walked through the spaces between them. If I took a photograph of the same tree every day—which I would like to do, if I remembered to—it would be about the taking of the picture, the process and the ritual, a way of marking the day and layering time, which is increasingly what the project of art is for me. If these photographs were ever viewed, the viewer would only wonder at the vast unknown of the day beyond the taking of this one daily photograph. All we can do is wonder over the imaginary solitude of others, what others do when they are alone, how they deal with the vastness and ephemerality of the day, which I think is for me increasingly the meaning of and crisis of art.

What Rilke desired was to discover the smallest constituent element, the cell of his art, the tangible means of expressing everything, like the sculptor with his disembodied hands. This desire for language to be broken down to its smallest elements—for a language to become a thing—mirrors the conclusions of the notebooks Wittgenstein kept while stationed on the front lines in the Austro-Hungarian army, theorizing the limits of language, what can be said about the world versus what can only be shown. The philosopher did not care much for literature, save the volume of Tolstoy's *The Gospel in Brief* he carried in his rucksack. He thought that it was impossible to express the mystical in language, so one should not even try, which is in diametrical opposition to the poet's searching. In September 1914, Wittgenstein, son of a steel tycoon, wanting to redistribute his wealth before he enlisted, gave the insolvent poet an anonymous donation of twenty thousand Austrian *kronen*, a fortune at that time. And yet the philosopher did not care for Rilke's writing, especially the novel, which he found excessively sentimental. The two were never to meet, and the poet never learned that the philosopher was responsible for this largesse. Rilke promptly spent the money on a new cream suit and on a new, younger lover. He was almost forty when he was drafted, brought back miserably to the bullying atmosphere of military school, although his patroness, the princess, arranged for him to be transferred to the war office in Vienna, personally escorting him from the barracks. Incapable of performing his task of writing fluff pieces on war heroes, he was reassigned to hand-rule sheets of paper for five months. This mindless labor is not what Rilke meant when writing of longing for work, that only on these rare days of work did he become real.

Before the semester begins again, what I can finally manage to read is Norman Malcolm's memoir of his friendship with Wittgenstein. Wittgenstein was not writing, he tells his friend, because his thoughts cannot sufficiently crystallize. I have increasingly become Dürer's melancholic angel, moving notes around and around, formalizing or finishing nothing. I have so little time left before teaching, so little pure time, and what I have I am squandering. Now there is a chance we might be moving for another library job for John. Always another listing for a job popping up that makes him envision imaginary futures. Or maybe we can figure out a way to survive in New York. We still consider getting a cabin in the country, somehow commuting in to teach . . . this conversation is constant between us. How to live, where to live, should we stay in the city, should we go and live in the woods? I spent the night weeping at the dining room table, I tell Sofia, worried over how to move forward with this book, just moving around my notes from the previous fall, attempting to arrange them. She replies to me that she was weeping at her kitchen table the exact same night. I was telling myself today, to overcome my intense frustration with how slowly my book is moving, that everything is writing, she writes me. That reading is writing, taking notes is writing, watching films is writing, copying is writing. Trying to extend all of these activities with equal intensity, so as to achieve a total experience of literature.

The last time I spoke to my father, I asked him whether the books I ordered for him had arrived, the first few in a Western pulp series by Louis L'Amour. He told me he was having trouble reading, he didn't have the attention span to keep up with his new history of mathematics. I asked what he liked to read as a kid, maybe he should go back to reading that—detective stories, like Dashiell Hammett, or Westerns. My father has always considered reading fiction as unserious, even though every night he watches at least one Western, sometimes more than one. Because I am also having trouble reading—that porousness where I make too many connections—I am only watching television on my computer. I try to read one of the novels by Norbert Davis, featuring a private eye and a Great Dane, because he's Wittgenstein's favorite crime novelist. I can't get past the first couple of pages. The opening line: "I'm in disguise. I'm pretending I'm a tourist."

To keep the dog still beside me in the office, I feed him drops of honey off my finger. I pick the sticky threads of goop from his eyes. To chart Genet's moodiness, how he wanders about the apartment—that seems like writing to me. I'm in bed, I'm not in a good space. A single line from Suzanne, canceling our planned chat. Don't disappear on me, I write to her, but she does, for long periods, she hides, or maybe I hide. The ones I love disappear, and I go chasing after them, and perhaps this is also why I am a writer.

Before I am to return to work, I finally find some clarity. It helps to listen to repetitive music on loop. And this brings me to gazing again, on a new morning, at the diptych of the paralyzed angel of melancholy and the Saint Jerome open on my desk. How they relate to what I am now thinking through, and how writing can reveal the depth and energy of thought. Before his spiritual self-portrait in *Melencolia I*, Dürer was so interested in idealized forms, in beauty and proportion. In drafts of his own text on beauty, *Four Books on Human Proportion*, which he was likely working on while conceiving *Melencolia I*, Dürer expresses a fragment of doubt in his notebook: "What beauty is I know not, although it adheres to many things. When we wish to bring it into our work we find it very hard." Both images, side by side, are beautiful, yet I am far more moved by *Melencolia I*. That Dürer has captured the silence of the room, and the cluttered act of thinking, of attempting to represent an inner experience. If I am to think of memory as a room, according to the medieval mnemonic, the mind then becomes a space as well, that can be either well organized and spare, or chaotic and crowded. Looking at the image of Saint Jerome, I think of how Wittgenstein wished for silence in his life, and how he would often go away somewhere, to a room sparsely furnished, in order to think. Sometimes a chair in a room was all he needed. And one can consider his resulting fragments as a series of empty rooms where each single thought is the only ornament. In his later *Philosophical Investigations*, he writes, "A person caught in a philosophical confusion is like a man in a room who wants to get out but doesn't know how." When I look at the two Dürer engravings side by side, I realize I am looking at two rooms, one half outside and mostly cluttered and in disrepair, and the other shaded with light, a sheltered, illuminated, comfortable, well-organized space. Perhaps the melancholic angel is an oblique self-portrait. The angel is the stand-in for Dürer's philosophical confusion, his doubts about the rules of art and the geometry of beauty he thought to be true. She is blocked—she is frustrated with the old forms, and wants to create new ones. His angel's dress is crumpled, she is hunched over, her hand on her face, perhaps deep in thought. Even the phrase "deep thinking" suggests a spatial aspect to thought. When I look at this image, in the middle of the night, I also go to Joseph Cornell at his kitchen table, in his mother's house in Flushing, Queens, working in the silence of the night, feeling paralyzed and stuck. Like Sofia and me each weeping at our own kitchen tables.

Sofia writes me that she has finally watched *Sans Soleil*. All the vibrations—the dancers and the animals, how painfully marvelous, she writes. Isn't it wonderful, I respond, how the piece travels, the technology of it, its trance state? All the shots of animals—the dog at the beach, the cat temple, the emu. Sofia writes me, I am trying so much (when life allows) to think about dissolving. A longing for this risky outward movement—like the risk Marker takes in filming Japan and Guinea-Bissau, or the risk anyone takes in writing about anyone or anything else. Rather than an identity that consolidates itself endlessly, an identification outward. Sofia writes me of the way she feels obliged to package the narrative of who she is and what she writes for this round of interviews for tenure-track positions. The exhaustion of expecting to chant, to belong to various groups and identities. But then there is the other group, the place where we meet, the eternal group, she writes, the radiant zeroes.

All I'm interested in lately, I respond to Sofia, is communicating through private letters or with the dead. She agrees. "Isn't that the basis of not only all art, but all religion? To have one's own dead. Who is more ours than Rilke?"

Although it's almost the end of January, yesterday was the first real snow. The way it lightly blankets everything reminded me of how I'm feeling lately. It is still sunny on our walk, and the two striped cats outside of the new cat house guard the spots in the sun. Whenever I see these particular cats a few blocks from our apartment I'm reminded of my little cat, because I think they must be related. I haven't seen her in some time. Yesterday I felt a seize of worry for all the outdoor cats in the snow. I coo to them when I walk by, laugh at their furrowed and stern expressions.

Today, after writing about my lost raccoon cat, I spy her. We're walking briskly in the cold when we pass the massive apartment building on the corner. A mother and her small daughter are looking adoringly at my little cat, curled up in a bush in a patch of sun. The mother is talking to her daughter about the cat, and the little girl is holding on to the iron garden fence. I stop and look at my cat, behind them, but then the mother looks back at me, and I feel I am bothering them, crowding their moment, so I move on.

When I saw the little girl clutching the low iron gate surrounding the garden, it occurred to me that the whole scene resembled a miniature zoo, and that my cat was like the lion sprawled out on the carpet in Dürer's *Saint Jerome*. Dürer attempted several times to draw a lion before actually seeing one in person. He used earlier sketches and prints of lions as his source, so they often look like large house cats. Even the lion in *Saint Jerome* looks like a wild cat, not quite a lion, napping side by side with the little dog, their paws almost touching, like a Renaissance version of those videos where different animal species become friends.

I read an article in the Sunday magazine about a sanctuary where abandoned parrots act as empathy animals for traumatized veterans. For weeks, I can't stop thinking about these parrots with episodic memory and theory of mind, who mumble and pace furiously or pluck away at their feathers as they recover from the trauma of abandonment, but are also still able to see others' solitude and pain. John sends me details of the parrots in a Dürer engraving of Adam and Eve. A caption from a biography: "In preparation for the return journey to Nuremberg, Dürer dispatched his trunk, had a traveling-cloak made, accepted many going-away gifts—including a third parrot, which necessitated bringing another birdcage—and settled his account with his landlord."

I see my new editor, an extremely smart young woman who is also named Sofia, a couple of months later out in the world. I am not sure what *Drifts* is about anymore, I tell her, but I know I want to write about dogs. And parrots. Have you read this article? I ask her, as I ask everyone, as I am apparently not properly socialized.

What is the *landscape* you're working in, I start to ask other writers, both students and friends, rather absurdly. A better question to ask, though, than What are you writing? or What is your book about? or—what Suzanne and I ask each other, quickly, lightly yet rather pointedly, when we see each other in person—Are you writing?

This weekend there was a great blizzard, about thirty inches of snow. We woke up Saturday morning with everything covered in white, like a bright empty field. While John shoveled I trudged around in my snow boots and took photographs of buried cars, of icicles hanging from the houses. Snow caps like silly hats atop the large lion statues. There was no pathway cleared from my house to the corner where the old woman lived in the yellow-and-brown house. By the time I finally got there, at the end of the weekend, someone had cleared the way to her front door. I wondered if that meant she was in town, as I hadn't seen her in some time. We often wondered if she went somewhere warm in the winter, or whether that was possible, in her state of seemingly genteel poverty. Although it's difficult to know with New Yorkers—she might hoard her money.

On one of our walks around large hills of snow, trying to convince Genet to go, an impossible task in the snow, I saw one of the striped cats. I had a feeling in my chest, a mourning for my cat, but knowing again that I was going to do nothing about it. Everything seemed to have disappeared in the snow. I watch the old man who wears socks and sandals in the summer talking to a young woman shoveling out her car in front of the house. I wanted her to tell him to stop bothering her, but she was too nice. I was surprised to hear him speaking with a Swiss accent.

At the beginning of February, sometime after the large snowstorm, we woke up to Genet growling, in a way that felt urgent and new. John thought the dog was dreaming and told him to go back to sleep. But then I became aware that there was an intruder in the apartment, though I don't know how. Now that I think back on it, I wonder if my nervous system had somehow merged with my dog's, as if I could smell or sense someone intruding in the house, moving around almost silently. John was slow to react, waking up in disbelief. I went to the door of the bedroom and realized there was no lock. I felt sure we were going to die. That this was it—the quiet before some unknown impending violence. I turned to John and told him I loved him. Although he still didn't believe anything was happening. When we finally opened the door and ran out into the main room, we saw the window in the kitchen flung open where someone had entered. The open back door where they escaped. Snow was blowing in onto the kitchen floor. Everything afterward happened so fast, and yet we were somehow still within it. I became aware in the minutes that followed—and how they stretched on—that only my belongings were missing. It was my laptop that was buried within the couch that was taken, while John's was left sitting on the kitchen counter, even though the intruder had entered through the kitchen. It was my heavy backpack that contained my new blue notebook with my notes for *Drifts*, most of which I had recently transcribed, except for the last week of notebooking. The old camera, too, was taken from a bookcase in the office, the one I had used as I wandered around in the blizzard, everything snowed under. It was as though the robber had set out to steal the notes and source materials for my novel. But what use were they for anyone? Why would he or they—maybe they were working in a group—have wanted that old camera, with photographs of lion statues and trees?

Since then I have wondered if perhaps Genet is not actually paranoid, if perhaps he is protecting us from unseen forces.

My laptop and camera were recovered, along with my phone and a pair of sunglasses. When the two police officers arrived, one of them turned on the phone-finder app, as my phone was broken and couldn't be turned off, and she tracked the signal to the contents of a backpack of a man they then arrested. He had dumped our bags by then and most of our belongings, including the notebook. We saw the man in the police station, in the middle of the night, waiting with us to be brought into a room for questioning. He looked at us and we looked at him, both rather blankly. We were told later that he was responsible for a series of cat burglaries in the area. How agile he must have been to shimmy up our window like that.

The next morning, having slept in the clothes I wore to the police station, I open the door to two officers, trying to keep Genet from humping their legs. They dust for prints everywhere, leaving a residue like fine ash. I am supposed to make my hand go limp as one of the men mashes into the inkpad with each finger, each tip, the side of each hand, as if I were dead. I can't do it. They show us photographs of their own dogs on their phones.

A few days after the robbery, having received a summons under our door, we dressed up as we would for a funeral. The self-consciousness of walking through the courtroom, feeling the grand jury watching me, perhaps watching the dress I was wearing. It was my only really nice dress, black, mid-length, three-quarter sleeves, sedate—my most respectable item of clothing. I repeated what the assistant district attorney had rehearsed with me, that I did not see the man, whose name has now been identified, but yes I knew there was someone in the house, yes I was frightened. As I sat there on the stand, my period suddenly began, and I bled with a gushing feeling into the only pair of good dark tights I had. I just sat there and bled.

We purchased all the items we could to replace what was not recovered. We thought this would make us feel normal, to have our things back, to be able to move on. I bought the same exact wallet, except in a different color. A similar winter hat and scarf. My makeup. I replaced my new white silk blouse, which was in the bag, as I had had a meeting that day with my department chair and wanted to look nice, and then spilled salad dressing on it. I felt like I was walking about like an impostor, with my impostor wallet, my impostor hat, my impostor scarf, my impostor white blouse. The same but not quite.

To replace the copy in my backpack, I had to buy a new edition of Hervé Guibert's *Ghost Image*, his book on photography, now with Guibert's beautiful face on the cover. I hadn't realized that before he was sick he looked like an Abercrombie & Fitch model, which unsettled me. I still had the photocopy of the pages I was going to teach, my passionately scribbled marginalia.

In the weeks that follow—weeks when I was unable to write, to record being an exhausted, legislated, bureaucratized body—I was most disturbed by the loss of the blue notebook. Also that so many of my identity cards

were stolen, though luckily I found my passport in a
drawer. A few days after, as we left the house to walk the
dog, passport in the pocket of my winter coat, we saw the
old woman from the yellow-and-brown house crossing
the street. I had not seen her for weeks. She was crossing
the street, and I waved at her.

I find on the camera the last series of photographs I took,
of the black-and-white cat who lives with the Japanese
woman and her young daughter across the alley. After
the robbery I would often find her staring at us, watching
what was going on.

I realize writing this I never used the old camera again.

The week of the burglary, an Italian moved upstairs, in the room above ours. It was as if he just suddenly appeared. He was subletting for the actress, away doing a play. The week after he moved in he knocked on our door, and, when we invited him in, he sat at our table and drank our bottle of whiskey. He told us that he was a performance artist and graduate student. He was enrolled in the same critical theory program as the photographer, which convened annually in Europe. When he saw a DVD of Gilles Deleuze interviews on our bookshelf, he eagerly asked John if he could borrow it. Technically it was mine, as it was sent to me, but I hadn't watched it. I told him I'd gotten lost recently on the Wiki "List of Suicides," as I was supposed to be writing an essay on Chantal Akerman for an anthology, and wanted to see if her name had been added to the list. I hadn't realized that Deleuze had died by jumping out a window. He started talking to us about Deleuze's long uncut fingernails, showing me a photo on my laptop—they reminded me of Murnau's *Nosferatu*.

He kept on knocking on our door late at night, wanting to hang out. We smoked his cigarettes with him on the front porch, in our winter coats. I asked him if he was the

one leaving out pancetta and milk for my raccoon cat—I
thought he might do something like that—but he said it
was the self-help guru. She doesn't leave her room, but
Skypes all day with CEOs, he tells us. I wonder what
she says to them, what she gurus. The Italian reminded
me of the charismatic boys I used to know, artist types
and intellectuals who were adrift. I am turned on when I
can hear him above us, shifting, moving things around,
when we are in our bed at night.

At the café, I see the Italian sitting with his theory books. I go over and say hello, but he is absorbed in his reading. A few minutes later, thinking I've already left, he sends me an email of apology. When he goes to use the bathroom, he sees I am still there. He stands in front of my table and starts telling me he is interested in stupidity and performance, like Chris Burden shooting himself. Or Vito Acconci masturbating in the empty gallery, hidden under a ramp, responding to the movement of visitors. I ask him if he's ever read Elfriede Jelinek's *Wonderful, Wonderful Times*, which he hadn't, and promised to leave out a copy for him on my doormat, as I had several.

After he leaves, I start to eavesdrop on a couple who seem to know each other but are seated at different tables, yet are carrying on with each other as if their conversation was ongoing or had been momentarily interrupted. As they speak I take notes in the margins of my notebook. They are both Russian. The body is an object, she asks him, or tells him, it's unclear. He agrees, the body is an object, but a person is a subject. So the dead body is an object, she says to him. Yes—a dead body is an object. Unless it's a ghost. But a ghost, she interjects, is a subject. So a ghost's a subject but a body is an object. Interesting, she says, I'll have to think about that. Then, at some point later, the woman asks: Do you think it's a crime if someone takes the object and does whatever they want with it? Yes, it's a crime, the man says. So it's a crime to have sex with a dead body, even though it's an object? Yes, he says. Why? she asks. Because it's the property of the state, he finally says. So the government owns us when we are gone, she says.

I have to leave because a couple has left their little Chihuahua terrified and freezing outside, while they sit inside, leisurely, and I become rigid and uncomfortable with my anger. At the same time I want to weep. Another woman locks her puppy up outside, but he escapes the halter and runs into the café. I go over and capture him, stroke him, while not looking his person in the eye.

When I get home, the Italian has sent me a link to a video of himself dressed up in a picnic table cover, writhing around. Isn't this stupid, he writes. I watch his body make specific gestures for some time. I don't email him back.

After the robbery, a constant feeling of dislocation. John takes me to see dingy cottages in faraway towns upstate. We spend whole days driving back and forth, stuck in city traffic. Yet we decide to stay in the same place, where we remain as I am writing this, gathering up my notes. Anna and I both abandon our country house fantasies at the same time. Was this fantasy, Anna writes me, a fantasy of not being distracted? But it was actually an elaborate form of distraction. The goal in life is to be still, Anna writes me, not to live a big life, but to be quiet and to write books, to continue to write beautiful books, great books. At least we aren't having children, she writes. Not only for the time. But because we will get our existential satisfaction from working, not from raising human beings. I wasn't sure if this felt true to me, I often didn't feel existential satisfaction from working, but Anna was always so sure and convincing in her pronouncements.

The problem, we decide, is that we can't focus, we can't go deep, we are always skimming the surface. I can't figure out how to work on the novel, beyond moving around my notes from the fall. I am so outside of the book, I write to Anna. I have awful menstrual cramps.

Should I take a muscle relaxer? If so, that's it for me for
the day. But I write Anna that, even when I'm disciplined and off screens, I cannot think all day, or I start
feeling overrun. Work for me is to *stop thinking* as well
as *thinking*, I write her. She appreciates how seriously I
take distraction, she writes me, viewing it as a problem
to explore rather than overcome. But how much of that
is just further procrastination? I don't know. How much
do I let myself take it easy, let myself be distracted? It's
uncomfortable to be in the space of a work too long,
just as it's uncomfortable being in the space of the day.
Once I get to the couch and begin watching TV I'm
done for, and I wonder if that's what I wish for. I crave
that relief, of nonexistence. It's the trance of worthless-
ness, Suzanne writes me. She encourages me to listen
to Tara Brach meditation recordings instead, though
I don't. Danielle sends me the same Tara Brach links.
I think of how Wittgenstein needed to go to the movies immediately after a class ended. He needed it like a
shower bath, he said, to bathe his mind after his lectures,
exhausted and revolted by them, by himself perhaps.
Genet is looking at me, waiting. I just took him out, in
my holey pajama pants—bleary-eyed, mind racing. He
takes forever to pick a spot. My winter boots sink in the
mud. The blue tampon applicator, the empty Magnum
condom box, a box of generic menthols, chip bags, all
blowing everywhere, petrified shit. Glass from a broken
beer bottle. How disgusting the trash is outside. A half-
eaten doughnut in the garden, a gold condom wrapper.
At one point G gobbles up a piece of shit, and I toe him

with my boot to get him to stop, just as someone walks by. The pizza boxes pile up outside. Some are ours, some are from upstairs. Dishes pile up. I haven't showered. I can't read. I can't leave the house. This fold of time I go into, as if lost.

That February, Anna writes me that she is fighting with her boyfriend, over how bad her housework is, how he tells her she is an eternal child. You are a great artist! I write to her. You are not supposed to be good at housework! I want to be a great genius like Woolf or Kierkegaard, Anna writes me, but I am worried that I'm not smart or focused enough. I've lost the ease in which I used to write, I tell her. I want to write books of moral seriousness, of history and memory, and I don't know how. I feel it's just outside of my reach, to figure out how. Every day I try to figure out how.

I don't think I want children, that relationship, I tell Anna, continuing our previous thread. But if all was thrown out the window—if I was told I could have a child when I was fifty, and I had finished a body of work I was finally proud of—maybe then I would. It's about time, and what we choose to do with our time.

Yes, a miserable writer can create great literature, Anna replies. What does a miserable mother create? Except alcoholic children, ha.

We meet up with the Italian in Chelsea in the freezing cold to go to an exhibit of Peter Hujar's downtown
photographs. All that year I thought about Hujar's
photographic subjects, often his friends, lying down, but
then also dying. Hujar's photograph of a young, sexy
John Waters. I confuse that image with my uncle on his
deathbed, as my uncle looked like John Waters in his
casket, once shrunken down to half his size. I also kept
thinking of that image of Wittgenstein on his deathbed in
one of the biographies, his sharp nose. Which I conflate
with the face of David Bowie, who had just died. And of
John Wayne's character in the casket with his boots on
in *The Man Who Shot Liberty Valance*, the Western I just
watched with my father. In the film both Jimmy Stewart
and John Wayne are in their fifties but playing young. I
am confusing all these men, lying down. I read, in my
Wittgenstein biography, how men in fin de siècle Vienna
were never taken seriously, so they took to growing thick
beards, paunches, strolling with walking sticks, wearing
gold-rimmed spectacles—all out of the desire to look
older. I save this detail to write to Sofia.

The Italian walks around with us to various galleries.
How many books have you written again? he asks. I can
tell he doesn't believe me. He asks John about writing instead. Afterward, we take a cab to a Japanese punk bar
and drink sake. When the server pulls out my chair, I
miss and fall to the ground, so hard that I have a deep
bruise for a month.

At first I found the Italian amusing, but as it becomes
spring I begin to find his attentions annoying, or possibly
sinister.

Suzanne writes me of her loneliness. She misses the intimacy of a partnership, of having someone to tell all her neurotic and trivial details. Email can feel so superficial, she writes me. I'm lonely, too, I write to her. Write to me, I tell her, write me all your neurotic and trivial details. She starts sending me letters in the mail, several in one week, which, becoming overwhelmed with other things, I never answer.

That feeling of ghostliness after the robbery. I still feel followed in every room—like a tracing paper over everything.

||

VERTIGO

Approaching the close of the nineteenth century, at a commercial photography studio in Prague, a child by the name of René Maria is photographed over the course of several years. To the modern viewer, young René Maria seems to be dressed as a girl. Boys in the Victorian era often wore full-skirted frocks with starched petticoats up until their breeching period, usually around four years old, or later if the boy was sickly, as was René Maria, born two months premature. The reason for this was partly practical and partly emotional. Pulling up a skirt made it easier to change diapers. The high rate of infant mortality meant that many did not survive past early childhood, including René Maria's sister, who died weeks after her birth, a year before he was born. It appears that René Maria wore dresses until at least five or six years old. Later in life, in supplicating letters that performed a lonely and traumatic childhood in order to ask for money or some pleasant accommodation—in a hotel, a sanatorium, a seaside resort, or a castle—the poet often repeated his personal mythology of a cosseting mother who dressed her delicate son, with the French feminine name, in girlish costumes well past the customary age. Gazing at the black-and-white photographs of Rilke as a small child is like gazing into a series of melancholy little rooms. Following the conventions of the period, the child holds a prop (a stick, a switch, an umbrella) and leans against a piece of furniture (a chair, a bench, a table), which helped to keep the subject still during the long exposure time. In Rilke's case, these elements appear incongruous, both spare and chaotic. As background there is either a blank wall or a painted landscape, which often creates the unreal effect of exterior blending with interior. One can measure successive years by René Maria's lengthening hair, curling about his neck, his skirted suit—front-buttoned for boys—worn with white tights and little black boots. In one session, held when he was four years old, René Maria wears what looks like a little straw pompon beret, and brandishes a switch. Befitting a writer for whom dogs would later provide tremendous solace, a rat terrier sits glumly on the small wooden chair where the child rests his tiny hand. In the next photograph, the dog is on the rug, alert, gazing at the camera, and little René Maria, hatless, holds a book bearing two cartoon drawings of animals, balanced against what appears to be a bench. In this session René Maria wears a bored, faintly melancholic glower that resembles the dog's. There is a feeling of endurance to these photographs. What has the child been promised in exchange for holding still? What complaints has he issued and how has he been soothed? The overall effect of these staged compositions, the strangeness of the surroundings, are like a mood. This artificial staging somehow conjures the solitude of being a child, the discomfort of the body,

especially in more formal dress. The one distinctive
element in these photographs that stands out, amidst the
hectic composition, are his eyes, the steadiness of his
gaze. There are two other photos of René Maria a year
or two older. In one, with a painted nature background,
he wears the same type of white collared dress and pleat-
ed skirt, balancing his elbow rather casually against a
molded wooden bench. In the other, he is dressed more
prissily, but with the same white tights and boots, with a
trimmed coat, clutching a frilly parasol and wearing a

pointed hat, in a room filled with heavy wooden furniture and a chair with velvet tassels. In this photograph,
with his pretty, pointed face, the hat obscuring most of
his fringe, René Maria hardly resembles himself. But he
stands on the same patterned Persian rug from previous

photographs, wearing the same white tights and sturdy little boots. As an older child, when he misbehaved, he would put on a dress and plead with his mother that he was no longer bad René but Sophie, his mother's name. He remembered how his mother liked to parade him in long dresses in front of her friends, like he was a large doll, and he spent hours combing his doll's hair, and putting her to bed. All to the dismay of René's father, who worked for the Austrian army as a railroad station manager and wanted his son to make elaborate battle plans with toy soldiers. Rilke later rewrote these scenes of childhood in the novel, although the fictionalized mother is rendered with softer light than in the letters— an example of what his hero, Charles Baudelaire, called genius as childhood recaptured at will.

Then there is René Maria at nine years old, dressed in
military costume, with polished, high boots, sitting on
a tasseled stool, facing the camera in his most asser-
tive pose. By now he had started at St. Pölten's military
academy, near Vienna, which he loathed for its brutal
atmosphere. The background of this photograph is more
difficult to discern—it appears to be a painted architectural backdrop, a palatial scene of grand moldings
and high ceilings. What is fiction, one thinks, but an
imaginary space? What is the imaginary landscape of
childhood, for that matter, but a fiction? Throughout
his life René Maria recalled his time at military school as
a torment. He told of being struck in the face by a bully
on the playground, and telling the boy, I will suffer this
as Christ suffered it, quietly and without complaint.
A martyr, fevered by the lives of saints. This ecstatic
obsession with death and mysticism would last his entire life. At the military school his sickroom becomes
a sanctuary, continuing the punctuation of illnesses
that would last throughout his life. His mother comes
to comfort him at his bedside. And here is René Maria
as a newly wedded man of twenty-seven, posed at his
desk in the farmhouse near the northern German artist's colony, in the first year of his marriage to Clara

Westhoff, before he left for Paris and a more itinerant existence. There is an aspect to his face, those eyes, their intensity, that retains something of the little child in all his manifestations. At the desk he looks like he's suffering, but perhaps that's the requisite stillness of having one's photograph taken. He has his new name now, a proper German one, the one that will make him famous, given to him by Lou Andreas-Salomé, his mother figure, lover, and intellectual mentor, though by the time of this photo she has abandoned him, disgusted by his sudden decision to marry. He will revert back to René Maria, not by choice, when he is enlisted in the Austro-Hungarian army more than a decade later, and then later again, when he immigrates to Switzerland. At the time of this photograph he has just recovered from scarlet fever, a month of fever and chills, his honeymoon spent at a sanatorium, this rhythm of convalescence following periods of work that characterized his adult life. Perhaps this period of intense illness, which weakens his borders between the past and the present, brought him back to the fevers of his childhood that he will describe so memorably in his novel, to the inner life of things that would later obsess his poetic thought, the destabilizing fear that the button on his nightshirt might be bigger than his head and the little woolen thread coming out of the blanket might be sharp like a wire. How illness stops time, how the body becomes a room for memories.

At the beginning of the spring, I find myself suddenly pregnant, which comes as a shock. I discover this after a long weekend of nursing John with the flu, and then feeling, curiously, like my insides were occupied by something else. The certainty and immediacy of the blue plus sign on the pregnancy test. How I suddenly began hyperventilating, and John made me breathe into a paper bag. And then we walked around, we walked around, buzzy, nervous, like nothing was real.

I spent those early days on the couch, dizzy, eating lightly yet constantly—fruit, beans, tofu, hard-boiled eggs. I lay there meditatively eating a banana. The fetus is the size of a lentil, the internet tells me. And then I eat lentils. Now it's the size of a blueberry, so that's what I eat as well.

I think I am enjoying my symptoms, I write to Suzanne, in those first weeks. Maybe that's a metaphor for life, she writes back, to enjoy your symptoms! She cried with joy when I first texted her the news. Sorry, I'm such a mom, she writes.

When I tell Anna, I can tell she is happy for me, yet full of ambivalence. She takes a picture of herself smoking and sends it to me: I was just vacuuming, now I'm having a cigarette on your behalf!

The paranoid space of the early-pregnancy internet. I google rates of miscarriage constantly. I lurk on Baby-Center community boards, crowdsourcing ambient worry. The gagging cutesiness of the acronyms: DH (dear husband). LO (little one). Now that it had happened, my DH was thrilled about a potential LO, which felt like he'd undergone a personality change, like he was suddenly a stranger to me. Maybe we'd both undergone a personality change. I, too, felt like a stranger to myself.

All I am supposed to do is wait. They say you can't be a little pregnant, but actually you can.

I've been in a fog of trying to write this book while also reckoning with an exquisitely tender and changing body, as if I am some sort of monster, I write to Sofia in March. Yesterday I walked around Wall Street near my doctor's office—Bartleby territory—and I could smell everything, as if I had a superpower: cigarettes, alcohol, shampoo permeating from skin and hair. The food stands. The train an intense, humid experience. I can tell what John ate for lunch just by coming near him. I wake up at night with a metallic taste in my mouth.

I think it's good to think of yourself as a monster while pregnant, Sofia writes back. I thought of pregnancy as the most natural thing in the world, because that's what I thought you were supposed to think. But I was in Cairo by myself during the day, and lonely and terrified, she writes. And also weirdly interconnected with everyone who has ever had a child or has been born or died. Overconnected, I found sometimes.

How nauseous and stoned I felt walking toward the
Canal Street Q, the way the green-lit neon fish crawled
slowly in the windows. I was reminded of the Sara
Driver film *Sleepwalk*, which I'd watched the previous
fall. Suzanne Fletcher plays a character who works at a
nocturnal copy shop in Chinatown, who is also tasked
with transcribing an ancient manuscript. Extreme long
shots of the Manhattan skyline. The city as a trance,
uncanny and floating.

Sofia sends me a Diane Arbus quote she found in her
notebook: "Everything is so superb and breathtaking.
I am creeping forward on my belly like they do in war
movies." I had written down that same quote, from
Sontag's *On Photography*, in my notebook the month
before. And I had just been meditating on a self-portrait
of Diane Arbus, young and newly pregnant, naked
except for underwear, in front of a mirror. Her head
cocked, regarding the specimen of her body, the brown
planets of her nipples, the slightly swollen stomach.

After a long day of teaching, weeping in the middle of
Times Square, where I had left the subway station because I couldn't handle the smells. Then at night, unable
to sleep. Should I have an abortion? I don't want one,
but I don't know if it's because I'm terrified of the procedure, yet surely childbirth is much worse. Having a
baby—the economics of it, the physical process of it—
feels impossible. But if I didn't want one, why was I so
strangely excited and worried before each blood test? I
don't know anymore what I want, or even who this "I"
is at all. This debilitating fatigue and nausea doesn't
help. I wanted a life devoted to reading and thinking and
writing—something like a monastic existence—and now
this is its opposite. I want to be in bed all day, but thinking and dreaming and taking notes. I want to be lazy and
selfish. I feel so apart from my hermit-bachelors, as if my
body has betrayed me.

The writers I know who are mothers tell me I won't
be able to write for the first two years. Or maybe,
even, the first four. My department head at the university tells me to spend the savings she assumes I have
on a nanny, like she did, if I want any hope of writing
or being my own person. This feels impossible. You've

already published so many books, and you're not even forty! Suzanne writes, trying to reassure me. Sometimes I think no one except Sofia gets this extreme desire of mine to transcend myself in this book. How close I feel to crossing a threshold to a new form. Yet Sofia is not optimistic about my chances of writing with a baby, or even a small child. I can tell she doesn't want to spook me. Only Anna assures me that I will still write, if I choose to go through with this. But what does she know?

Sitting in a paper gown yesterday, left waiting for two hours, my feet in stirrups, I said out loud, to the empty silence of the room, "Seriously, I have to work on a novel."

Naps that are midday crashes, which leave me melancholy and dreary after waking. My body feels swollen, alien to me. Could Kafka's *The Metamorphosis* be read as an allegory of pregnancy—a body that's suddenly unfamiliar, the nausea, the small hard stomach, not being able to get off one's back?

I spend hours one afternoon trying to coax my little striped cat into a box so I can take her to the vet, who's agreed to foster her. She appears to be nesting. I worry that she is pregnant. (Of course I do.) Our dogwalker sees me outside the apartment building next door, trying to capture the cat, and says she saw a larger raccoon cat rape her a couple of weeks ago—that's the word she uses, "rape." People stop and comment. Two women with a little dog who live in the building tell us that they call her their cat too, that they feed her tuna fish. Today she comes right up to my hand and sniffs it. I look into her beautiful green eyes. She is getting larger. Later, the scene from the fall repeats itself: the same mother and daughter come up to her, at the building gate, and watch her sleep in the garden, as I watch them watching her, keeping my distance.

It is now spring. Tulips and irises. I sit in a chair with a blanket on my lap. Genet asleep on the rug, the windows open.

One of the notes I take that spring: "vagueness." Another: "signs."

Breakfast in Sunset Park. People carrying palms after church. Then driving through the Purim festivities in Williamsburg. Circles of inebriated men wearing hats and costumes out of the nineteenth century crowding into the streets, slapping shoulders. Children on the sidewalk dressed in more Halloween-like costumes. Little girls with full faces of makeup. In that moment I feel buoyant, like I can leave my sick body. I think of Kafka, his love of Yiddish theater, the electricity of the amateur. I could have watched and watched.

I flip through a novel recommended to me, by a living male novelist, entranced by dead male novelists.
How suspicious I am of myself, how I have clung to the
canon of the bachelor hermits, I write to Sofia. A canon
that so often doesn't allow space for us. Sofia writes
me that she wishes sometimes she'd stop reading men, but
that it would be like cutting off half of herself. She gets
angry, too, at the pressure to talk only about writers like
herself, from the outside, as opposed to other writers she
also resembles, from the inside. The truth is, I have often
lately wanted to occlude all identity and community—to
disappear—but I understand that there's a privilege to
that, or worse, a purposeful erasure, I write to her. She replies that she'd love to withdraw from race or gender, but
that there's very little space for that that doesn't support
troubling politics, so we wind up reifying these identities,
again and again. We have had this same conversation, on
loop, for more than two years. Perhaps it's seasonal, this
affliction. We are irritated when we're on lists. But then
of course irritated when we're not. Like all these constant
panels on women's writing, I write to her. Yet why was I
not invited to this one?

Although we are always ourselves and others, all the time, Sofia writes. You are always the diffuse and ghostly "you." Aren't you still a woman when you're reading Kafka?

The Italian and I are often the only ones in the house during the day. On Wednesdays, he talks loudly on Skype for his long-distance graduate program. We are doing feminist theory this week, he tells me in the walkway as I'm leaving with the dog. Virginia Woolf! he says. Cixous! It's clear he wants to talk to me about his reading, but I am not interested in talking to him. Later he sends me a message, asking if I have more women writers to recommend. I click the button blocking him.

I'm a *novelista*, I tell Beatriz, pointing at my cluttered desk, as she stands over it with me and tries to dust the top of my books, my notebooks, my printer. She doesn't seem to care (why would she?), but she is very excited to discover the photographs from the ultrasound on my bookshelf. I didn't know what I was supposed to do with them. She effuses over these splotchy black-and-gray photos. We drink coffee together—one of the two tiny cups I'm allotted daily, which I siphon out religiously. I ask Beatriz about the Italian. *Loco*, she says, and I agree. He won't let her inside his room at all. I wonder what's in there. What kind of stupid bachelor mess is inside.

Crashing out on the scratchy sofa in another temporary office, in between classes. This semester, at another college, I have been occupying the space of a scholar of early American literature who is on sabbatical. A poster of an impressively bearded Melville, crossing his arms as if defiantly. On the door a postcard of Edith Wharton, holding her tiny long-haired Chihuahuas on her lap, Mimi and Miza, like spooky twins. Her childhood nickname was Pussy (I just googled "Edith Wharton" and "Pussy" while cringing). I sit at the scholar's desk and try to force myself to eat the parts of the salad that I can manage. I open her desk drawers, examine the crumbly beige circle of her powder compact. I walk around and look at her walls and shelves while willing myself not to vomit my lunch. Framed photographs of her lacrosse team from college and her study abroad at Oxford. Her cap and gown regalia hung up. Her family on a beach posed in identical white T-shirts with rolled-up denim—all smiling and blond. A framed crayon drawing.

When I go to the café near my house, I watch the mothers at the outside table with their toddlers, sharing a pastry. It alarms me, the claustrophobia of this romance. To be alone all day with a child. To be tending to their thoughts, not one's own.

I learn that I can manage not to vomit when I go out into the world if I am constantly eating sour candy—as sour as possible—and my stomach is never empty. I bring a sub sandwich to my classes, cutting it up into multiple portions, and slowly eat it over the course of the afternoon along with two bags of sour-cream-and-onion chips. I try to ignore the message boards, which tell me not to eat deli meat, because of listeria. Sometimes I rush out of class to throw up in the bathroom. My students don't realize I'm pregnant. They probably just think I'm gross.

In the spring I see Clutch when they are in town. Maggie
Nelson's *The Argonauts*, which came out last year, is still
all anyone wants to talk about. We joke to each other,
we need to cowrite a book about hormones, the estrogen
injections they're taking, my pregnancy hormones, but it
will be about how fucked-up and weird hormones make
us feel, it will be radiantly pessimistic.

Never have I orgasmed like this, so rapidly and repeatedly, even though our occasional sex is missionary, per-
functory, because I am so sick and uncomfortable, except
for this. Perhaps for once evolution giving the pregnant
body some pleasure, to help with the misery. The satu-
ration as well of my pregnancy dreams. So much sex and
death.

In April, a Swedish newspaper wants to profile me because of a new translation of a book I wrote years ago. The morning of the phone interview, I vomit up a green smoothie with surprising recoil. I'm not quite sure what I say to the reporter. I don't feel like the same person who wrote the book she wants me to speak about. And yet I know, I wrote the same book from the same body as I have now, the same yet eroding set of memories or past, just as this stomach is the same stomach as when I was a child, and as it was a month ago, and yet how it changes, regenerates, stretches, transforms. During the interview, I find myself on a rant about Knausgård— that I can't believe that Sara Stridsberg's novel on Valerie Solanas had not yet been translated into English, I'd rather read that. I resented that I was supposed to read him. I resented his sexy leather jacket and his sexy leather face. Hanging up the phone, I imagine the inevitable pull quote, and feel somewhat ashamed.

The Swedish newspaper also wants me to meet a photographer at Chelsea Piers to get my photograph taken. I feel nervous about this, as I am bloated and my clothing has mostly stopped fitting me. Since it is still cold, I figure I can just wrap my long black robe coat around me, the new coat that I've just purchased for half off in a winter sale, that probably won't fit me for long. It doesn't matter that I got my hair cut and styled for the occasion—the wind is so fierce that in the photograph my hair is blowing around me, as is somehow also my skin. The photographers say they want me to be outside, since I apparently spoke about my longings toward the flâneur in the interview. In the photograph they choose, I look bleached-out, uncomfortable, not myself. I think of the moment in *Camera Lucida* when Barthes describes getting his author photograph taken, experiencing "a kind of vertigo—something of a detective anguish."

The next month, I am invited to a gala celebrating Semiotext(e) at Artists Space. At the party, I talk for a while with Chris Kraus, who was my editor on the book that had just been translated, until she finally realizes who it is she's been talking to. You don't look at all like your photograph, she finally says, referring to the Swedish newspaper. I don't know how to respond. The truth is that the photograph doesn't look like me, and also that I no longer look like me. The invitation said "black-tie formal," so after much worrying that I had nothing to wear, I wound up spending too much on a long black jersey dress with bat-like sleeves, a minimal necklace. It's stretchy, I reasoned, I'll wear it throughout, and even afterward. But it doesn't matter anyway—Eileen Myles is there in jeans, looking so totally themselves. I wind up telling everyone at my table that I'm pregnant, I have no idea why.

It is interesting being known mostly in Sweden. The book is reviewed widely there, even in major newspapers, but it's all in Swedish, and so I don't have to read it. It is a relief to google myself and for the results to be incomprehensible. Perhaps it's all really about someone else—it has nothing to do with me.

On my nightstand, Clarice Lispector's extravagant face stares at me from the jacket of her collected stories. I manage to read only one story, about the saturated sadness of a mother of small children, "the secret center which was like a pregnancy." The young woman spends an afternoon in bed, then wakes up still having to peel the potatoes and wash the clothes. Then she goes out at night and gets incredibly drunk, the alcohol exuding through her flesh. A word from the story: *gravid*, meaning pregnant or full of significance. I open Sei Shōnagon's *The Pillow Book* but can't read past the beginning, the description of the dog being beaten.

Oh yes, Bhanu replies to me. Total blankness. No reading or writing. I didn't like it. Finally, I could read: Maeve Binchy's romance novels set in Ireland.

I spend my spare time thinking about the pale yellow fur coat with white dotted trim that many of Vermeer's women wear in his paintings. I page through plastic-coated books that John brings me from the library. The light of Vermeer's paintings. Their silence and mystery. So often a woman writing at a desk or reading a letter. How ordinary they are. So often the painting seems to be of the same room, at the same picture window. John and I look at the images together, thinking of what time of day is depicted in different paintings—whether the sun floods in directly or diffusely. He takes the day off so we can go to the Met and to the Frick to look at their Vermeers. At the Frick, one of the yellow-coat paintings: the mistress and the maid look over a letter. On a nearby table there is a large vase of lilies, the smell overpowering the room. I feel dizzy. I sit in the tropics room, a sort of glassed-in courtyard, the water rushing, and stare at all the green.

Looking at the Vermeers, I am reminded of my conversations with Sofia from the fall—how to empty a text in order to fill it.

How unsettled I begin to feel in tight spaces. The claustrophobia of this dark apartment. The claustrophobia
of my body. By the end of April, however, I begin to
feel a little more human. I begin to find the riot of flowering trees and tulips less ominous and overwhelming.
I sit out on the porch with the dog and drink my little
cup of coffee and write in my little notebook. I begin to
dream of landscapes, of escape—of land art out west, of
European cities. All that spring I think of how Joseph
Cornell didn't travel, traveling only in his works.

It is now May. I have only the summer to write the novel, but in the mornings especially I can endure only the strange labor of my nausea. Still, I sit outside on the porch to get fresh air, notebook at my lap, the dog at my side. By late morning, the jackhammering will begin next door, and my thinking will end. The next-door neighbors are building out a back patio. It's cold out, but at least there's sun today. It's been so gray. For weeks— so gray. I felt some quiet and green walking the dog this morning and want more. I dream now of the country.

Last week I saw the baby, on the monitor, swimming inside me. Afterward, I broke down weeping in the entryway of the hospital, overwhelmed by the new certainty of my life. There was some part of me that thought this wasn't real, that this wouldn't be permanent.

Outside on the porch, letting Genet sprawl in the sun while we watch the men carry concrete back and forth, pile rubble in trash bags into the green monster of a trash compactor. I caress my dog's little rump. Outside it feels more possible, to return back to my notebook, to reading and thinking. Everything inside feels muggy, chaotic. John killed a large cockroach this morning. He has locked himself inside the bedroom, moaning, sick with the stomach flu. A few days later, I will be the sickest I will ever be in my life.

In my inbox, results from the blood tests, the news that we are having a girl. I sit here and think about this—a girl. What does that mean? Does it mean anything? Should it? Something sorrowful and profound about it. Thinking to the isolation of my childhood, of that child, and everything foreclosed from her, so soon. Like my daughter—my daughter—is now doubled inside of me.

These copies of days. The metronomic quality of summer. On the porch Genet goes in and out of light and shadows. Porch time, John writes me, your necessary nutrient. I want to buy a straw hat today. Maybe a dress. To feel buoyancy. I look up at the glowing canopy of green— the trees above, the birds. Finally I pick up my phone. Texts from Suzanne have accumulated while I was sitting here. She writes to me to avoid writing to him. Our little fragmented missives to each other, trying still to check in, even while living so far apart. I want to write about the prickliness and fragility and beauty of this friendship someday, but I don't really know how. I never want to betray her.

I've managed only this one paragraph in the past two hours.

I begin to experience something like extreme pain over the flyers of lost dogs and cats, pasted on the street lamps and sign posts in my neighborhood, near busy roads, the descriptions heartbreaking in their specificity.

Was it in spring or summer that we drove by Prospect Park and saw a dog running from the sidewalk into heavy indifferent traffic toward the park? The pace of its run, as if delirious with freedom. I made John drive around and around. I felt sure it had been hit by a car— but maybe it ran into the park? Maybe it was captured? I didn't write any of this down in my journal. It stays in my memory as a jolt—a sprint across those months, across these pages now.

There are two types of irises in the garden, a deep velvet maroon and a lavender with a yellow center. I don't love them but appreciate their tallness, their certainty. I have become aware of time again, of the cycling through seasons. Genet rolls over and I scratch his belly with my dirty fingernails.

It seems the workers will be here all summer. Beefy and tattooed men appear, wearing baseball caps bearing American flags. They shake hands. They yell *Yo!* at each other. Is this a big job today? They carry garbage bags of debris, cigarettes in their lips. I think my presence unnerves them, this pregnant woman with her little dog, watching them.

I know I will be a completely changed person, I write to George, so I have to write *Drifts* now or never. His wife is in her third trimester. I've been writing and reading frantically, he writes to me. I have been doing nothing, I respond. Like a dog or a cat.

And yet today I feel I can summon the will to write the book. Outside feels so much more possible than inside. Even the internet—that's inside.

Today I saw the old woman directing two men carrying a new stove wrapped in blue plastic from a truck into her house. She was dressed too warm for the weather, in wool slacks and a thick turtleneck. This was my second sighting of her this week. This spring we'd seen her wandering around on a parallel street, unable to find her house, which she asked us to point out to her, which we did, although we then went home and worried over what we should do, if anything. How much more I worry about her now. How much more I worry about everything.

Yesterday a sighting of the striped cat as I walked to the train, her little raccoon tail skirting under a car on our street. A quick puncture of joy and relief at this.

The two women in colorful veils taking their morning walk always smile at me now. Perhaps I too have become a recurring figure in their landscape, but it may also be that they find something about my appearance pitiful now.

Genet's shits are so slow and particular in the afternoon. The feeling of it in my hands through the plastic bag. The beauty of his little asshole, how it expands, like a flower.

I hope you don't think I've been ghosting you, I write to
Sofia from bed, cramping from the amnio. How sorry I
felt for myself after the long needle, the crummy paper
cup of juice and package of cookies they gave me afterward, as I shuffled into the waiting room where they
could watch me to make sure I didn't faint or miscarry,
then shuffled home on the subway, sitting through the
jolts. I've just been a ghost in general. I was recently invited over to the Soho loft of Marie, a writer from the art
and fashion world who once interviewed me. Not having
made many friends here, and feeling so lonely and anxious, I wrote her that I was pregnant, as I knew she had
a small child, and she invited me over for lemonade. I
wore what I thought of as my most chic black tank dress.
I was starting to show, even though it was early, and I
felt so monolithic and sweaty next to her—her slender-
ness, her glamour, her caffeinated energy. It turns out,
she whispered to me, she was very newly pregnant with
her second. Immediately she invited this intimacy with
me, which made me feel flattered and hopeful but also
nervous. There was someone else there, an artist I had
met before—I hadn't realized it wouldn't just be the two
of us. I would come to learn that Marie often had someone else with her, usually a male artist or collector type

wearing expensive sneakers. Sitting at her table, sipping lemonade, I started telling Marie about the burglary, and the artist intervened, and began lecturing me for calling the police. He told me that once, when he'd had an intruder in his apartment, he merely chased him away. And, Sofia, I still don't know whether he was right or not, but it was his tone, his insistence that he knew what was right and I had done something wrong—and that our situations were the same—that irritated me. I began, for some reason, to tell him about my project, that I was spending the summer thinking through this drifty essay on time and the body and looking at Dürer and Vermeer. And he kept on interrupting me, But how are you connecting this to the contemporary? To what was important, I think he meant. And, Sofia, I don't know if I am. I don't even know why I listened to him. After seeing him, I couldn't write for days.

I have to turn in this project at the end of August, Sofia, and I'm paralyzed! I'm just fluttering on the internet constantly. Worried about the editors who are considering the mother book. Worried that feelings of rejection from that project will further stop me. All I can read now, when I can read at all, is Flaubert's *Sentimental Education*, and I underline all the descriptions of food and clothes: the twelve types of mustard served at a dinner, the hero's "pair of pearl-grey trousers, a white felt hat, and a gold-headed stick."

Of course a haunting like you are writing to in *Drifts* is exactly *not* about the contemporary, it's about the contemporary being interrupted, Sofia responds to me. I feel that there is a rightness to it, to what you're haunted by, and that it is not in fact separate from the body. This body that is only asked to speak on "gender and feminism." The bruise that we have spoken about so many times before. The Bartleby.

And yes, the twelve kinds of mustard—I completely understand! My problem is that I want to just revel in the objects, just be ravished by the surfaces of things. I think I told you before that I couldn't write when pregnant, could not read anything but Agatha Christie, Sofia writes me. I had a huge stack. And I'd watch old black-and-white Egyptian movies and cry. There was one about an orphan girl who gets taken by these horrible people who cut all her hair off. I cried so hard! And I'd take the ketchup from the fridge and smell it. It smelled amazing.

Sitting on a lower step so Genet can lounge in a patch of sun. It is cool out today. My belly has really appeared this week—I cannot easily curl up into a ball, or masturbate on my stomach. I am hunched over in my striped poncho and straw hat, scribbling in my notebook. The dog has now found his corner on the porch, blocked in by the Adirondack chair. I bask in his blond-gray Sontag streak, his liquid amber eyes. I scratch the top of his head, scratch his little gray goatee.

Yesterday I posted a photo online in my new summer stretchy dress—that Yves Klein blue. This is the best you've ever looked, Anna writes me later. You look so avant-garde, how pregnancy suits you. I'm really struggling, I write to her. As if in reply she sends me a draft of her manuscript, but I can't bring myself to read it.

In the night, sleeping on the couch, not being able to bear being with another person. Everything feels out of control, I write to Suzanne—I am feeling my isolation deeply. I am sure the hormones are partially at play. And also the stream of rejections of the mother book. And my rage and grief toward the hierarchy and casual cruelty of family that this pregnancy has catalyzed, that I thought I had clarity and distance from. I want my father and sister to be loving and present in a way they are not capable of. Also John is gone eleven hours a day, and the days feel glued together. I watch screens when I'm inside. I spend days not speaking to anyone but John. I feel like everybody has abandoned me. The privacy and alienation of this pregnancy, like an illness.

After one of these borderless weeping sessions, I am ghostly and numb the next day. I realize, I write to Bhanu, I am more worried about the milk, about afterward, than about the birth. How would it feel to be drained that way every day, by another person? How intensely emotional it will feel. I don't yet feel prepared for it, for that form of love, for all of my love to leave me, to fill another so completely.

How long I can exist on the porch, surrounded by notes. I'm reading another Rilke biography. How slowly I read anything in this heat. The impossibility and desire of working on Rilke. The vertigo of another's life, of reading. I can't really work, but I stare at the bobbing chickadees. I want to take photographs of the roses growing on concrete, in tiny gardens of apartment buildings, straining against wire fences. Perhaps because of the roses, because I'm attempting this study of Rilke, the same line of his keeps circling in my brain: You must change your life. This is what I'm most scared of—but of course it must happen. I pull Genet's warm ear. He starts at the bugs.

I am beginning to think that the woman in *Melencolia I* might be pregnant.

It is now June. I write to Bhanu today that I have been thinking of the extreme interiority that Lispector conjures in her work, but I cannot bring myself to read more stories. I sometimes feel closer to the books we carry around but cannot read, I write to her. She is reading the biography, slowly. Bhanu tells me that she spends most days writing strange things. Maybe for a chapbook. I ask after her teenage son, as she's mentioned on her blog that he has been sick and she was on bucket duty. He's better, she says—now they are arguing because he hasn't brought in the neighbor's trash can. I write to her that a few weeks ago I, too, was sick with a stomach bug—I couldn't even keep water down. It was after I recovered that I began to come to terms with being pregnant.

I want to write increasingly small and minor texts, I write to her. I've been reading a biography of Rilke and am thinking of how he viewed art as sacred, how it was necessary to refuse the exigencies of the day, how he felt bored when he met his baby daughter at Christmas, he didn't want anything to disturb his writing life. I feel so far away from this. Bring me the exigencies of the day, I say. The garbage can and the neighbors and the vomit and the slowly read Lispector. I am far more interested in that.

The last time Rilke was with Lou Andreas-Salomé, they buried her beloved poodle. In a postscript to a letter, he asks whether the dog's replacement, a poodle named Schimmel, recognizes his smell on the envelope, and she replies that he gave it a good sniff. (Poor Schimmel would die two years later; Lou Andreas-Salomé had bad luck keeping dogs alive.) At this point, in the late summer of 1903, they have been estranged for two years, and he reaches out to her, as she'd told him he could do so, at his true hour of need. From a friend's house at the artist's colony in Germany—where he's staying with Clara for the next two months, recovering from the exhaustion of his illnesses and from the city—he writes to ask if he can visit her. She suggests that they renew their correspondence first by letter, and in response he begins his urgent epistolary, narrating his past year in Paris and the details of his convalescence. He is unable to write about his suffering, he writes to her, except in these letters. Sometimes he writes her so frequently that she doesn't have time to answer, and he wonders whether his letter has been lost in the post. He writes her from a damp, melancholy room at his friend's house, blocked from light by the tall trees. It is not the room he usually is given when he is a guest there. Since their relationship has aspects both maternal

and clinical, he writes to her of his remaining symptoms:
poor circulation, hemorrhoids, toothaches, eye aches, a
sore throat, fevers. He has tried steam baths and walking
barefoot in the garden wearing his blue Russian tunic,
despite the gloomy rain. When he lived with her, in
Berlin and the suburbs, he kept her strict work hours,
which made possible her prodigious output of novels and
tracts. Days spent studying and working except for their
barefoot walks in the woods. He adopted her way of life,
her peasant dress, her vegetarian diet. After complaining,
Rilke is given his usual little red room, which faces south
and gets better light. In all these years, he writes, he's
never had a quiet room, this is what he's been looking for,
a room that no one else enters. The solitude is imperfect:
the dramatics in the garden of the couple's year-and-a-
half-old daughter, the same age as his own daughter,
who is two hours away on a farmstead with his wife's
parents. A new baby, the second child, is due any day,
cutting his stay short—infuriating Rilke, who must now
go to his in-laws. How far away his painter friend, with
his pregnant blond wife and cozy domesticity, is from art
making. Everything about his world has gotten smaller
and smaller, his house contracting around him, filling
with the noises of the everyday. His art, too, has suffered
from it, has become vague. He finds himself filled with
unease amidst life's casual unthinkingness. Nothing un-
expected can happen with all of this dailiness. For everything must go into the art, he is sure of it. One must
choose: either art or happiness. He remembers that first
awkward déjeuner with the sculptor and his wife, how

overcooked the meal was, how chaotic the table. (Rilke, a picky vegetarian, had written to Clara complaining that he didn't want to eat anything.) The photograph of the three of them posed with the couple's two shaggy dogs, standing at the pavilion in front of a collection of antique headless marbles. The sculptor and the poet in black heavy coats, Rilke petting one of the dogs, the squinting sculptor's wife in her long black frock. It was during that awkward, unappetizing meal, he writes now, that he realized that Rodin's house was just a roof over his head, a wretched necessity. Deep inside of him, he bore the shelter and comfort and darkness of a house.

There was a time when he'd thought a house, a wife, a
child, would make his life more tangible. But now he
wishes to withdraw more deeply into himself, into the
monastery inside him, replete with great bells. He would
like to forget everyone, forget his wife and his child. One
must live within one's work and stay there. Only once
life has become work can it then become art. We are not
made to have two lives, he writes passionately in his irritation, there can only be one. And yet he is unable to
focus, to get anything done that resembles work. Is his
will sick? Does he lack strength? Days go by and still
nothing happens. He cannot become real. That is the
fear, he confesses—he cannot become real. A silhouette
in the midst of bodies, a fiction in the midst of reality. He
wishes to cling to something when these fears come, and
it must be work, and the things that work can produce.
Once he had pined for the everyday world, for the visible reality, for people and a house that belonged to him,
but now he sees he was wrong—it can only be *things*, he
repeats. Only things speak to him. All this he writes to
his correspondent, in a breathless confession. She replies
with details of a quiet concreteness: Schimmel the poodle
staring hypnotized at a squirrel scrambling up an old tall
linden tree in the garden.

How melancholy Genet is when he wakes from a nap, his
chin on the rim of his blanket basket. I spend the morning trying to organize my notes from the fall—it's going
badly. I hear from Sofia, who is reading Walter Benjamin.
Today, she writes me, she arrived at his sentence, "Then
what's the point of writing?" and then stopped.

Trying to write a book with a baby moving inside me
feels so strange. It reminds me of Kathy Acker telling students to write while using a vibrator.

My stomach is big. It's not fat—it feels like some whale-
bone construction in there. It's hard to move around with
it. People open doors for me now. I look like a pregnant
nun in my blue dresses, a strange performative feminin-
ity. I've been trying to figure out if the women posing
for Vermeer's paintings are pregnant. This one who is
reading a letter in front of a window, could she be his
wife? Perhaps these were just Dutch fashions of the time.
Although Catharina bore him fifteen children! She was
probably always pregnant. Eleven survived.

We go to the country for the weekend. John takes my
photograph in panorama on his phone in the On Kawara
room at Dia:Beacon. In the photo, I'm surrounded by
dozens of his date paintings. My growing belly traces the
passage of time.

Every July, Beatriz goes home to Peru, to drink from the sap of a local tree that helps ease her ailments, her aches and pains. She's now been diagnosed with diabetes. I tell her, each of us communicating with each other in our halting ways, that so many on my father's side have had limbs removed because of it. I whack away at an imaginary leg with my hand. She shows me the map across one slim muscular leg—a dog bite on her thigh, the varicose veins on her calf. She shows me a bandage on her arm where blood was drawn. I lift my shirt and show her my belly. I'm too *gorda* for five months, she says to me, which coming from her I don't mind. Last time I saw her, she told me that many she knew had miscarried at four or five months, I had to be careful.

All afternoon I have to keep Genet from humping her leg. Beatriz waves him off, laughing. Animals love me, she says. She tells me she has several cats, a few dogs, and a cage of canaries at home.

Why is the baby always the size of a fruit? A lemon, an orange, an avocado. Now a cantaloupe or an artichoke. Or potatoes or a banana. A kitschy calendar of the body. John notes that these fruits are all randomly sized. What if it was a squirrel? he jokes. Your baby is the size of a squirrel.

At the hospital, the moment I realize that everyone is pregnant. The uncanniness in the waiting room.

I have not changed out of my short white maternity nightgown all day. Anesthetized by window-unit air-conditioning. Genet moves around to various rooms. We've gone outside for only minutes today. So gray and hot. I did not recognize anyone on the street. Genet would only pee. We both felt spooked.

The new assistant district attorney who is handling the burglary case has been leaving messages. They want me to testify when there's a trial, which will be in my third trimester. We don't return his calls, and every time there is a message I feel nervous and shaky the rest of the day. The man who robbed us is apparently still in jail awaiting this eventual trial. John finally talks to the ADA over the phone—an investigator for the defense might be knocking on the door, asking questions, pretending she's not connected with the case. Since I've spent all month binge-watching *The Good Wife*, I expect to see Kalinda, the investigator from the show, in her leather jacket at my door.

They finally stop calling probably once they realize they don't need us to lock him away. It isn't about you and him, it's about him and the state, the ADA tells John, when he complains about how much time they're asking for, once he tells him that, if I was compelled to testify, I would be a hostile witness. How guilty we feel about this, but we don't know what to do.

Every night we watch an episode of a British spy thriller, and then I have nightmares revisiting the robbery. I was up for hours last night, convinced I'd heard a noise. I attempted to slow my heart rate down by going belly to belly with the dog. The other night I woke up and panicked that the linen dress hanging on the door was a shadowy man.

Neighborhood drama involving the frizzy-haired woman
with the green vest who is always walking her trio of
rescue pit bulls. We routinely see her stop people in
the street to lecture them on how to walk their dogs.
We've learned to ignore her. Last week, while walking
Genet, John heard a high-pitched scream. When he got
close to our apartment, he saw the Polish woman holding her Pomeranian limp in her arms, while the woman
with the frizzy hair was trying to talk to her. One of her
pits had apparently attacked the little dog, who ran up
to them—off its leash, of course. It becomes the talk
of the neighborhood. Was the little dog killed or just
injured? We have to find the owner of the Pomeranian
and find out what happened, I text our dogwalker, Mya.
The Polish woman has not been spotted since then—
except when John saw her later that week at the Duane
Reade, looking distraught. Mya texts me that the woman
got out of her car the other day and chased her down the
street, demanding she stop lying and telling people that
her dog had killed the little dog. She has now been leaving long and threatening messages on their Facebook
page. She needs a psych evaluation, Mya texts me. I
cringe, thinking of how we speak of women we perceive
as unstable. Still, her dogs are large and aggressive. The

murderous row, I've taken to calling them. I feel pity for them, but that doesn't keep me from picking Genet up as soon as I see them ambling by, refusing to make eye contact.

I'm writing a murder mystery, I've started to tell people.

My father and aunt are in town, so I arrange to meet them for dinner. They don't ask questions about me, how I'm feeling, what I'm doing with my time, what I'm writing, but I know they want to see my pregnant body. At dinner they tell me about a book they are both reading, about the history of cancer. Always so morbid, the two of them. But I've been also thinking of Wittgenstein's prostate cancer, Rilke's leukemia. I had just been writing Sofia of the nineteenth-century practice of deathbed memoir, dictated to the dutiful daughter who lives with the patriarch. How erased I feel after I see family, my eroding sense of self. How many days—weeks—it can take to recover, to feel outlined again.

Two photos yesterday I took with John's phone, even though I haven't wanted to take photographs lately: One a decapitated Barbie doll stuffed in a plastic bag under the wheel of our parked car. (Is it paranoid to wonder if someone placed it there?) The other a hole in a tree in the park more than a mile away where birds built a nest out of blond hair, seemingly from the hair of the same doll.

On a Friday, I want to stay in bed all day. John lectures me that I have to worry about time. Are you telling me to practice self-care or to work? I ask him. Both, he says. I throw my wooden clog at him, which cuts his hand. We are both on edge, underslept. Up the night before, throwing off covers, shining a flashlight on the sheets. Realizing that the brown bug we saw on the dreary hotel bed for our weekend away upstate had left itchy patterns of bites on his arms and neck, my leg and foot. How gray and hot it is outside, the constancy of this. We have begun to fragment by the instability of our lives here. Now a job in Chicago John wants to apply for, even though I have painstakingly lined up classes for the year. Also the national mood—the constant grief and stress. It feels impossible to leave the bed, so paralyzed by all the news. The horrors stockpile and there's no way to filter them. Headline: The emotional toll of a violent news cycle.

I don't leave the house except for brief hot walks to take
the dog out. I have begun to walk around the apartment
in a T-shirt, without underwear. I tell Suzanne about my
fights with John, my recent depression and regression after
seeing my family. She texts me her own feelings of isolation and abandonment, encounters with her ex. The partial
ways we keep in touch. The way we retreat and withdraw.
Clara Rilke complaining to Paula Modersohn-Becker
about how housebound she feels while pregnant, and then
with a baby, how impossible it is for her to get on a bicycle and pedal away. Paula miffed at this, feeling that Clara
has abandoned her and their friendship in her marriage,
how dare she complain. That photograph of the painter
and sculptor as young women. The women in white, Rilke
called them. They stare at each other, so complete and con-
spiratorial. I email Suzanne the photo. That's us, I write.
How it makes me weep to think of Paula, who died so
soon after childbirth, just when she was at her full potential as a painter. How close I feel to crossing a boundary
in my work, and then how stopped as well. That line from
Adrienne Rich's poem about Paula, a rejoinder to Rilke's
unnamed requiem: "They say a pregnant woman dreams
her own death."

Still, in all of this, the occasional beauty of encountering strangers. Their kindness and tenderness. I shower, finally, and walk to the nail salon. I haven't had a manicure or pedicure in months, unable to bear the smell or tedium. I tell my manicurist—Pema, she's Tibetan, from Nepal—that I am pregnant. She asks me how I am feeling. She, too, felt incredibly ill the first four months, like she was dying, she says. This was with her first child, a boy, now ten. They live down the street from us. With her second, who is two, she was fine, normal, she says. With her first, she could eat only potatoes or white rice. No one tells you this, I say. Being a woman is not nice, she says then, slowly, in sympathy, gently massaging my hands. She tells me about a friend of hers, who while pregnant was so nauseated by the green color of her rug that she chopped it into pieces and threw it away. As Pema is telling me this, she is painting my nails a silver glitter, like a prom dress. I tell her that for a time I couldn't stand flowers, the bulbousness of flowering trees. So strange, she says to me. I agree.

Feeling stoned on a bench at the botanic gardens. I had
the idea of venturing here on the train, to luxuriate near
a blooming bush, writing in my notebook and thinking
about Rilke's roses. Try to be with flowers, large arrays
of flowers, Bhanu had written me, when I wrote her of
my recent depression. Try to be inside flowers. Instead
I staggered through the browning rose garden, already
overheated in my denim maternity overalls. The passive-
aggressive performance on the train now. People know
they should give their seats to me, but I feel I'm supposed
to act humble, Madonna-like in my gratitude. I sit on the
bench and watch. Robins looping up and down. A few
tourists. Women with strollers dot the cherry orchard.
This is who comes here during the week, I realize: Mothers. Nannies. A way to leave the house, to be outside.
The security guard lingers near me. In the rose garden
I had asked him the way to the closest air-conditioned
enclosure and he had pointed me to the nearby business
center. Now I am stuck here on the bench. Perhaps he's
concerned that the obviously pregnant woman might
faint. There's construction noise, even here. I can't escape it. School groups wearing identical bright T-shirts
in case of separation. A couple strolls by, both on their
phones. I am more wilted this trip than I'd imagined.

I watch a bridal party pose for a portrait against a tree. I think of a massive hybrid oak I'd taken a partial picture of when ambling into the park. In a fuzzy, indistinct way, I connect this with a line from Agnes Martin I'd recently scribbled in my notebook, from the back of her biography I hadn't yet read: "When I first made a grid I happened to be thinking of the innocence of trees and then this grid came into my mind . . ." Agnes Martin in her denim overalls.

I look at the women with babies strolling up and down the cherry orchard and wonder if I'll ever feel uninhibited again. Whether I'll have true solitude again. I wonder whether I have it now. It is so unknown to me. The notebook is how I think, and see. My fear that I won't have it anymore. I used to see this army of strollers as intrusive, but now see the vulnerability of how these women occupy public space. Women gaze at me and I don't know what they think I am, or what they think I represent. How one of my department heads, the medieval scholar, just wrote to me over email: Happy Baby Waiting. Like that's what this summer would be for me. Even though I'm a writer—even though she hired me to teach writing. Also that she was amazed I still wanted to teach next year, that I wept and begged to be offered a class again.

I also don't understand the bounds of this new body. The security guard still watches me. Afraid perhaps I've gone into a fugue state. Which maybe I have.

Later I manage to get up from the bench and walk around the gardens. At the Japanese pond, staring at the slow turtle and large orange fish. Overheated in the tropical orchid room. Then finally at home in bed, white food stains on my black nightgown. I take off my militaristic bra, which leaves deep red grooves on my body. I drag plates of food to bed—bagels, cold pizza. Genet waits for my scraps.

I wake up feeling hungover. Weeping when John leaves.
I put a dress over my unshowered body and walk slowly
through the humidity to go eat an omelet on the patio of
the local restaurant, despite the heat. The constant hunger,
as if I'm a zombie. I refuse to cook; I can't handle the smell.
I am now completely unworking. Even at the restaurant I
keep texting with John, unable to bear my own solitude.
The melancholy is overwhelming.

And yet there is an intense beauty, if I allow myself to be
present in my sadness. How I am seeing colors. The purple
flowers of the butterfly bush. My orange-red toenails. My
new dress, a magenta linen caftan. I wear it the next day
when I go into Midtown with John. My plan is to read Rilke's
letters at the library but again have no proof of address. Me
in the vestibule, the contents of my bag scattered, trying to
locate ID. Instead I go to the art and architectural room and
read Rilke's monograph on Rodin and copy some of William
Gass's introduction into my notebook. Whenever the poet
went to the Bibliothèque nationale, he felt overwhelmed
by research, copying down everything he read. His constant
search for a space where he could work. It wasn't possible in
the grand reading room, even with the light pouring in from
the great oval leaded glass, the stacks all around him.

The garden is wild again. Daisies, echinacea. I text an image to John of the dog lying in the sun. John agrees, Genet does look like Rilke—the heavy, begging eyes, the downturned face and mustache. (Or does Rilke look like a dog?) What a strange and beautiful mongrel, he writes. I eat a mealy peach and feed a bite to Genet from my mouth.

The little dog lazes at my feet.

Still, the little dog lazes at my feet.

The relief of turning my mind off and watching TV on my computer. The trancelike nature of the Kardashians. Kris Jenner tells her daughter Kourtney that she is reading a book about the Swiss architect Le Corbusier. "I'm reading a book. It's so weird and boring, but I'm obsessed."

It's summer, so my friends are writing or away. My correspondences have dried up. Although still my inbox crowds with requests—to blurb or be interviewed, or to do this event or that—now with these awkward asides about my pregnancy. How lonely and private this process feels. What process do I mean? Writing a book or pregnancy?

I write to Danielle today of my intense desire to make beauty out of this drift. A way to experience time. It's not that life is less important than writing, I say, at least for me it's not. . . .

I've begun avoiding the office, even though it's the coolest room. Genet pads in here gratefully and settles on the small slip of white rug. I take a photo of my desk— my neon Post-it notes, the Dürer book open, postcards, photographs, notebooks, and send it to Danielle. I suppose I will have to give up this office, soon, for the baby's room.

After a few days I hear from her. How tender it is, the need to have space to write, whether it be the need for time, money, a pen name, or silence.

This is not a heat wave, but a heat dome. So much to write down, yet it is all so hazy. I cannot leave the house. Genet lazes in his patch of light—I watch his breathing move his body up and down. This morning he ran into my arms while I was still half-asleep—I caught him as he was heading for my pillow—because John was trying to kill a moth in the kitchen. What a guard dog.

I have not seen the old woman from the yellow-and-brown house in quite a while. Is she stuck inside, has she escaped?

I wake up with a pink eczema patch on my cheek, because of last night's pint of ice cream. I wait for the encroachment all over. I exist on the couch now, covered with my white patchy food stains. In the morning I balance my oatmeal on my pillow. My breasts falling out of this long black nightgown, which has now ceased to fit. My new dark brown nipples are the size of silver dollars. So odd—that my body can transform into something else.

I am barely conscious in this heat. I like that I can see the tall yellow daisies from the garden through the front window, even when Genet reclines on the radiator. In the morning he is wrapped in the cheap white gauze of the curtains, like a little bride. I give him the orange bowl as I lick the spoon. I wander around during the day tripping on yogurt containers I have set on the floor for the dog to lick. I realize I've been drinking from a jar of water that previously held the dying flowers from the farmers market.

Lately I have been thinking of the relationship of my body to time. How time moves this summer, so slowly and quickly, how my growing body keeps measure. But also how my body has become a measure of time for others as well. Although I dread the public comments on my body. I never anticipated how many unsolicited confessions I'd receive from people I barely know or don't know, about their ambivalences and desires and histories surrounding children and pregnancy. I receive them all, in this humid state, without really responding.

Genet is at his regular perch, looking moodily out the window. We are listening again to the shifting timbre of the man screaming in pain.

Yesterday, wandering around the apartment in my sleeveless chambray dress like the ghost of my grandmother, in her hot kitchen, my belly huge. I feel as if I've been caught within a Vermeer.

After constant wavering as to our plans, and always on the verge of cancellation, I meet Marie to see the show of early Diane Arbus photographs at the Met Breuer. She insists on taking a car uptown, paying for it, which makes me uncomfortable, as I almost never take cars, but I am sweaty and exhausted from the train. Because I always dress carefully to see her, I wear an off-the-shoulder white jumpsuit with an exaggerated saclike silhouette that I bought at a boutique. I wanted my maternity wear to make me look like a glamorous alien. I wander around the show and think about the anonymity and intimacy of Arbus's photographs of others, that queasy line that makes them so thrilling. That a photograph was the stilling of an encounter. In a letter, Arbus wrote about her photographs: "They are the proof that something was there and no longer is. Like a stain. And the stillness of them is boggling. You can turn away but when you come back they'll still be there looking at you." Marie wants me to take her photograph in a full-body profile, to announce her newly sloping belly on Instagram. I am already huge and she is still so slim. I feel clumsy following her around, trying to surreptitiously snap her photograph, as cameras aren't allowed.

After an absence of two years, Rilke returns to Paris to act as Rodin's secretary. Paula Modersohn-Becker is staying in Paris as well, having left her husband to try to live the artist's life. She begins to paint a portrait of the poet, but René Maria distances himself from her, not wanting to take sides, and the painting remains unfinished, as she dies suddenly the next year. There is a stark hauntingness to his blue unfinished gaze in the painting. At the beginning of his novel, his character relates that he is learning to see. He doesn't know why, but it all enters him more deeply, and nothing remains at the level where once it used to be.

Before, when Rilke went to the Louvre, he'd found it too full, everything was disturbing, he felt like he was disappearing into the crowds. Now he finds he can see certain pictures, he can actually appreciate the beauty of the *Mona Lisa*, as if all of humanity were contained within her infinitely tranquil portrait. Now he feels fully outlined, he writes to Clara, like a Dürer drawing. His hatred of the city has shifted onto his fictional double, although all he can do is take notes on his character's fate, which consumes him. He leaves on a lecture circuit for his book on Rodin, from whom he has now become estranged.

Back in Paris, he stays first at the Hotel du Quai Voltaire, where Baudelaire finished writing *Les Fleurs du mal* fifty years earlier, but soon moves to a cheaper hotel on rue Cassette, where Paula Modersohn-Becker had stayed before she moved back to Germany to have her first child. It's obvious now, he thinks: He must be in the city, he must see art. He drinks milk at his favorite vegetarian restaurant on the boulevard du Montparnasse to fortify himself. A painter friend, one Miss V., brings him a portfolio of Van Gogh reproductions. Even in his most exquisite agony, Van Gogh could paint his hospital's interior, he marvels to Clara. And the sculptor—even when he's not feeling well, he can still draw, read Plato, he still lives the life of beauty and of the mind, he still can follow this joy. And yet Rilke himself remains so far from being able to work at all times. He wishes he had no plea-surable memories of not working. Hours spent waiting, flipping through old illustrations, looking at some novel. If only it were enough, he writes, to have a dog and sit in front of a shop window for twenty years. In October he goes several times to the Salon d'Automne at the Grand Palais, returning again and again to these paintings of

Paul Cézanne, the hermit from the countryside who made paintings of an indescribable radical colorfulness, paintings of attention and beauty that were deeply inspiring to Paula Modersohn-Becker when she saw them in Paris. Now heavily pregnant and back at the artist's colony, Paula reads his letters along with Clara. They could not afford for both of them to be in Paris, so Rilke describes Cézanne's paintings to Clara. He makes saints out of ordinary objects, and forces them—forces them—to be beautiful, he writes his wife, the sculptor. A friend observes of the hermit painter's work, that he sat looking like a dog, without any nervousness, without any ulterior motive. At the Louvre, looking at the Venetians—what must Cézanne have thought of the colors of Titian, Tintoretto? Rilke begins to look at Paris through this painter's eyes. He sees the autumn as if painted on silk, and the yellow of the books of the *bouquinistes* on the quai, the violet brown of the volumes, the green of the portfolio, all this lyricism he later lifts for his novel's opening. He writes of this painter as a shabby old man, exhausted, seized by rage, like the old white-bearded man of Tintoretto, waking at six in the morning to walk through the town to his studio, the local children throwing stones at him. He would paint until ten o'clock, return along the same road for lunch, and then return to the studio to sit in front of the painting and his objects for hours, leaving only for a nature walk, and then bed at six in the evening, on the edge of collapse. Does Rilke see the irony of romanticizing all of this to his wife, whom he has left alone with the child and the domestic, so that she cannot get her work done? The sculptor or the painter, with their dutiful spouses, the modest constancy and poverty of their studio and work lives, the sameness. To be monastic is to be unmoving—it is what Rilke left behind, for he was a different sort of angel, the peripatetic, the courtly poet, the constant traveler who refused humble lodgings, always searching, *grasping*, longing.

At the cabin, after three days of driving across country, my body in burning discomfort while trapped in our tiny Honda. We had to stop every two hours for me to stretch my body and empty my bladder, after downing so much water to prevent the false contractions that come with the extreme heat. Sick of public bathrooms—of wiping down seats, of the cheap toilet paper getting stuck in my pubic hair, of waddling my sore body through doors of identical highway rest stops. I hold Genet on a pillow on my lap, as he agitates at bridges and rumble strips. Disturbed by the looming MAKE AMERICA GREAT AGAIN! signs, as we drove through Pennsylvania, through Ohio, through Michigan, like ominous humid beacons that we couldn't quite believe.

At the cabin I sit in the cushioned rocker my grandmother would sit in, because of my burning back. Through the window we watch the dog scamper off leash. What a noble creature, John says. I feel close to something here. Perhaps to nothing, that's what I'm closer to. The ephemerality of this pregnancy, like this summer, a sort of boredom or rapt interiority that doesn't translate into work. John hands me a plate of cut apples, almonds, cheddar cheese.

It's now noon and I need to nap. John drinks a beer and we watch the dog play. "Country TV," he says, as the dog takes off, running after his first chipmunk. We go to the dock and dangle our feet in the water. I rest my head on John's back. The slowness here. I needed it spiritually.

Now we are propped up in bed. Genet lies between us,
farting freely. The long yellow legal pads where I copy
out everything in the Rilke biographies. John reading his
biography of Walter Benjamin. There are no pressures
here, John remarked to me earlier today. I gave him a look.
He amends his remark: No pressures of the day, nowhere
to go, nothing to do. But he realizes my deadlines—my
book, my body. Your beautiful parasite, he says, kissing
my stomach. She worms inside of me. I like that phrase,
"beautiful parasite." That's what an artist is to me.

It is now raining out. As John strokes the dog tucked next
to him, I suck John's cock, the taste of it earthy and warm.
He takes the dog into the other room while I pee, and we
fuck in the bathroom, against the sink, John behind me,
me watching us in the mirror. We've had to try new positions to get around the belly. I watch myself—finding
beauty now in my reddened skin, my crooked bottom
teeth, the gray hair in my curly mop, my blue veins in
these huge milky breasts, these red-brown nipples like
abstract paintings.

We sleep in a cabin surrounded by forest. The lake is still. Last night I listened to an owl in the distance and wondered whether I will have silence again, afterward. On the morning walk I am slow and overheated. Later John puts a cool washcloth all over me to cool me as I sit down to drink some water. The constant labor of hydrating and eating. I go for a swim in the lake. How I welcome the weightlessness of the water.

Even with the peacefulness of this week, so much obsessing over what we will do when the baby is born. Where can we afford to live, how can we afford childcare, how do we afford John's unpaid paternity leave. How will I continue to teach through my last trimester, and how will I teach the following semester, with a newborn, even though I've agreed to three classes on three campuses, panicked about money. Perhaps we can attempt a Rilke year—a cheap farmhouse upstate. An intellectual sanctuary, John says. He wants to be home, to not miss the days our fathers missed. He wants to paint and to write about art. A monastic life. I want it too, with him. To be guardians of each other's solitude, like the Rilkes. Yet they, too, were always so worried about money. It didn't work out for them.

Back in the city. I haven't seen my cat all summer. Sometimes I think I see her tail swinging around the corner
or underneath a car, but don't know if I'm hallucinating.

It alarms me, how large my belly is growing. I can't see
my pubic hair any longer. I feel I'm running out of time.
Maybe Rilke was right about the impossibility of sus-
tained work in the summer. My belly is so hard and sore.
It's 7 p.m. and it's still so airless outside. I'm wearing my
orange hippie tank dress with nothing underneath.

I cannot turn *Drifts* in at the end of the summer. I have
had to beg for more time. The fall, I promise, before the
baby is due.

It is now the end of August. Anna writes me that she's
confused about her book, which she's still rearranging.
She can't tell if it's off and bad or close and good. She asks
me whether I've read it yet. I tell her I haven't been able
to. I'm extremely pregnant and uncomfortable, I write to
her. She tells me in return that she's been in bed for two
days with a wasp bite on her foot, how badly it's swelled,
how itchy and painful. How phobic she is of deformity,
she writes. How awful, I write, balancing my laptop
on my belly, trying to be sympathetic. She's packing to
leave soon for two weeks. A literary festival somewhere
international and cosmopolitan. We talk about how much
we've both been spending on skin care. For her, lipsticks
and sheet masks. For me, an expensive deep blue balm
for my pregnancy eczema that I smear on my face every
night, a calming ritual.

She sends me a photograph of Elsa Morante at her
desk, morose, chin down, staring at her books. That's
me, she writes, except in bed. I send her links to Paula
Modersohn-Becker's self-portraits. Later, when I ask how
her foot is feeling, ask when she's leaving, she tells me
that she has begun reading Modersohn-Becker's letters.
She asks me if I want to go with her to a publishing

conference in September. That's a hard pass, I write to her. Yeah, I don't want to go either, I don't know why I agreed. She's been reading the letters of Hannah Arendt and Mary McCarthy, and that she thought of our friendship, our intimacy and forthrightness. Which one is Hannah, and which one is Mary? I ask her. We decide that neither of us is either of them.

Genet lays down hot on the wooden floor outside my office so he can watch me. He is waiting in protest for two hours before his lunchtime. I take him outside quickly, just avoiding the murderous row.

I see her frizzy hair bobbing outside my window—I realize my hair looks like hers now.

I keep on receiving the same voice mail message from a number I don't recognize, which makes me panic every time. *Emergency situation. Go into lockdown now.* It is from the college where I haven't taught since the fall.

On the porch, eating a large bowl of overripe melon, staring at the garden. I am attempting again to organize my notes from the fall. Genet sits on my foot, a protective measure. He then circles around, not knowing where to slump. The sun has traveled to the far corner of the porch, where the wood is rotten. I call him back over, stroke his soft ear, a soothing gesture for both of us. The garden is so overgrown—there is almost no path to walk past—yet our landlord has once again cut down what remained of the butterfly bush.

Inside I watch the short film Agnès Varda made while she was pregnant. *L'Opéra Mouffe*, in English *Diary of a Pregnant Woman. Par une femme enceinte.* The opening shot of a naked pregnant body, the contracting of it, the clever juxtaposing shot of a large gourd being sliced open, the scooping out of its insides. Walking around rue Mouffetard. The filmmaker is watching the old women at the vegetable stand talking energetically. Staring back at those staring at her.

Apparently my uterus is now the size of a pumpkin.

The French word for "pregnant," *enceinte*, also means "border" or "enclosure." The enclosing walls of a fortified place. How secret a pregnancy can feel and be, how internal and private.

The other day I saw the old woman outside on her chair on the porch. I crossed the street to say hello. Enjoying the sun? I asked her. Enjoying the shade, she replied. She was wearing her beige trousers, the pink oxford shirt. Has she been inside all summer? Have I?

Today I saw a striped cat with green eyes and a raccoon tail on her lawn—it looked exactly like an older version of my cat. I fear my little cat is dead.

Last night in the warm (not hot) bath, we saw the baby moving under my skin. I turn over to my side and let John cup handfuls of water over me. Genet has taken to giving cursory licks to my nipple when he greets me in bed, and when he stands up to kiss me at the edge of the bath as I bathe every night this week (only lukewarm water allowed), my back aching. John wonders if my nipples smell different now.

I saw the woman in her chair again this morning, in her white robe and nightclothes, with what looked to be the newspaper. Me void-like in all-black linen. I waved at her with two hands. I wonder if she's noticed by now that I'm pregnant, if she remembers me at all. I like your doggie, she says to me, a recurring phrase. John and I hold hands, are very affectionate.

How noble Genet looks in his big-cat stance. Genet just went berserk at the postal worker as he was bringing an Amazon box for the Italian, who apparently lives here again, having returned to sublet the actress's room in her latest absence. I forced Genet back on the porch, picked him up, despite his resistance, and kissed his face and chest and belly—trying to calm his nervous system against my own. And now he is stoic again.

The larger striped cat, the doppelgänger, stands in our path on the sidewalk, in front of the big house with the exquisite garden. It looks so much like my cat, I fantasize that the wealthy residents have adopted her. Maybe it is true.

Days spent complaining online about my lack of maternity leave and writing long emails. Rilke complaining of
not writing despite the volume of his correspondence.
I can't seem to work on the Rilke story—it has stalled.
I don't know how I'm supposed to narrate his life. I am
sitting on Genet on the couch—or wedging my massive body against him and pillows—as he freaks out at
the large moving guy who keeps going in and out of the
house. The self-help guru is moving out. I will miss her,
her ghostliness.

Everywhere I go in public someone has a comment about my body, or unsolicited advice. The man who cuts my hair asks me question after question: What parenting style, astrology sign, name, gender, will I have a vaginal birth? I smile, I respond. Why do I answer? Most of the answers I do not know. He dyes my hair dark, like the swatch of fake hair I pick out for him; he cuts my hair into a more manageable bob. I don't like it. But I just want to feel in control somehow.

There are tender, intimate interactions in this public space. I go again to Pema, the woman who painted my nails. She asks me how I'm feeling. But mostly I am a throbbing, public thing. I miss anonymity—privacy— the ability to wander around. That I had actually become invisible was a relief to me.

That's right, you're pregnant. The Italian is tan and slimmer, back from Rome. I am sitting on the bench with the dog. He gestures to the notebook on my lap. Are you writing? I'm curt with him. I just want him to go away. He has probably heard my weeping sessions this week, panicked and stressed about money, the future. I don't know how my body can handle the commute to teach in the fall. The bureaucratic tone of human resources at the college upstate, telling me I don't get any official sick days or leave when I go into labor near the end of the semester. Finally soothed over the phone by the head of that department, who has always been kind to me, reassuring me that I can miss a class or two, under the table. He had recently published a novel from the point of view of an aging feminist, to some acclaim. How humiliating this all feels, this constant prostration. It is like one of Kafka's novels, John says to me—they won't tell you what you need to do, and any proposed solution is met with nonresponse. The university also tells me I must make up the class, but they won't tell me how.

How precarious my life feels now. Will we move, will we stay here, will we have to welcome it, to see possibilities in it, not foreclose ourselves? Maybe we belong here, in this city. Or where else? How will I continue to exist, to write? I feel almost mesmerized by this sadness lately. Maybe I should have gotten an MFA or PhD, or written the kinds of books that would have won prizes and awards, like the ones that fill the bios of the faculty I'm reading with next week. Another faculty reading. How can I still have nothing from the book to read? It's so fragile, private, unfinished. I don't even know where it's housed. But also it's within me, unbearably intimate. Like my other uneasy tenant, swimming around inside of me.

After a morning of commuting uptown through Times
Square (the raw heat, the stairs), of obliterating encounters and meetings at the university, I peeled my black
dress off my sore body and climbed into bed with Genet,
curling around him naked. I wept, as he licked the tears
off my face, until he left to throttle his stuffed penguin
in the next room. Later I think of a work by Moyra
Davey, a photograph of the artist pregnant and naked
in bed with her terrier, collaged with the line from Anne
Sexton: *Why else keep a journal, if not to examine your
own filth?*

The office I'm sharing this semester at the college upstate belongs to a poet who has won a multitude of awards and also appears to be somewhat of a hoarder. Boxes of papers everywhere, various phones not in use, thermoses, empty containers of laundry detergent lined up behind the desk. A whole row of Rilke on her bookshelf. I take home an out-of-print biography. (I'm realizing just now that I've never returned it.) The poet comes in with a student assistant, as I'm speaking to two potential students. I am awkwardly positioned on her couch. I'm sorry, who are you? She's never heard of me, even though I've been teaching there five years. What do you write? she asks me. She catches me off guard. Prose, little things, I stammer out.

It reminds me of when Lou Andreas-Salomé took Rilke to meet Tolstoy at the turn of the century. On the brief walk the master agreed to, he ignored the young poet, speaking in Russian to her instead, until at some point he finally asked the younger man, what was his occupation. I have written some things, the poet managed to say. Which was true. At that point he had written the few books of verse and the lone dramatic output of his alter ego, eternally twenty-eight, alone in his dingy Parisian walkup.

Today in the accessibility seating on the train, during the crowded rush, an older woman, dressed sedately in black, takes out a bottle of nail polish and begins to touch up her nails. A shimmery brownish-pink like my mother wore. The smell is overpowering. During the entire ride back to Brooklyn, I try to figure her out. So professional and closed in on herself, but unaware of the fumes she gives off, or indifferent to them, which bespeaks something like exhaustion. Her tidy yet worn wardrobe, black orthopedic loafers, black cardigan, and black trousers. Pearl earrings and a gold watch with little diamonds around the face. A black Michael Kors bag. I decide she works at the Macy's at Herald Square. In watches, or leather goods— why her nails must be impeccable, why they chip, tapping on the glass case.

Yesterday on the train I observed an elderly couple across from me, eating a bunch of lychee-like fruit with hard brown shells, shapes I've noticed piled sculpturally on stands in Chinatown. I watch the woman peel back the skin, putting the pieces back in the plastic bag, while spitting the black seeds on the floor, like glossy stones that skitter near my feet. The fluidity of that gesture. All without saying a thing. I watch again, as if everything is in slow motion.

Up late with night sweats. My body radiating heat. Up again (slowly, sorely) at 4 a.m. John strokes my flank, trying to soothe me. Time feels now so fast, yet I cannot believe I have to carry her, in this city, on these commutes, for two more months. When can I feel weightless? Last night, instead of a heavy dinner, I had a small bowl of the new strawberries. I ate them cold and freshly washed, my feet up, rubbing them together.

On my day off, I stay in bed. Overhot all day. I share my raspberry sorbet bar with Genet, even though it tastes fishy afterward. I try to avoid the Italian when I go outside. A woman coming out of the apartment building smiles as I lumber after Genet. He shits little ribbons because of the heat.

As soon as I get home from teaching I strip off everything—everything feels too restricting. I eat a sticky bun while sitting on the couch without underwear. I remember the grocery store coffeecakes on the plastic tablecloth in my grandmother's dining room—how hot it'd be in the summer, my grandmother refused to install an air-conditioning unit. This weekend we saw Vera from the dry cleaner's being pushed in a wheelchair, a cast on one leg. I stopped and asked her in dismay what happened. She grasped my hands, her fingernails long and unpainted, and something in that reminded me again of my grandmother, the way she cackle-laughs, her asking when I'm due, exclaiming, It's a girl! It's a girl!

The cat is back. I almost cried to see it. Such a little thing—she wagged her tail slowly back and forth and walked a few blocks with me. Are you walking with your cat? a man asked me. She is my cat! I wanted her to come to the porch. I put out cat food and water while Genet barked at the window hysterically. I am so happy to see you! I said to her.

Sofia writes me that she dreamed of her abdomen sticking out. Everyone lately is writing to tell me they've dreamed about me, or about pregnancy. The emotional weight of being asked to carry other people's dreams. As if I'm some harbinger of anxiety. Every day I'm a little larger, my clothes a little tighter. She swims around and around inside me.

I write to Sofia that I don't know how I came to be so pregnant, but I'm sure it's linked somehow to the robbery.

In early September, instead of reading birthing books, having also canceled the birthing classes, in order to try to work on *Drifts*, I watch the early films of Chantal Akerman. I was asked to write about her for the anthology exactly a year ago, an essay I have now failed to deliver. I finally feel able to enter her films again. The slowness of her work. The camera skirting around the room in *La chambre*. The repetition of claustrophobic interiors. I take notes on my own domestic space. Going to the fridge to get food. The fruit flies. Genet following me. Clothes hanging on the drying rack. The clutter of books and notebooks. Heating pad and pillows on the couch.

I take photos of the screen while watching Akerman eating sugar in *Je tu il elle* and think of restaging it. Where can I get a mattress in a room? I text Marie. Perhaps she will art-direct it for me. Anything you need, darling, she writes back. Although she is pregnant and miserable as well. I will write letters and shovel a bowl of sugar into my mouth. That's what I feel I'm doing anyway. Of course I soon forget this—it was only a momentary desire.

Together John and I watch Akerman's *News from Home*, eating cashew cheese nachos on the couch, Genet curled up on my left hip, wanting the warmth of the heating pad. I have to get up constantly now and change positions like the dog. The camera tracing the young filmmaker's walks when she lived in the city, working odd jobs in the early seventies. The opening shots of large American cars, transit depots, the neon signs of diners. The forlornness of the mother's letters, which the filmmaker reads in voice-over. "I hope it's not too hot—I know sunny weather depresses you." Her mother's complaints about bad health. "I thought it was menopause but it seems it's exhaustion." The ghostliness of these letters, the absences we feel in between, how so few are returned. The maternal longing, guilt, worry, chastising. The gossip and news. Engagement and birthday parties. Money worries. Vacations to the seaside. Babies born. The soothing repetition of her address. Darling daughter. We project onto the daughter's silence—she is experiencing the alienation of New York City, this new, temporary home. The exterior shots are the postcards she does not send. The spaciness of such a work. Night. Windows. The geometry of the train platform, extended long shot in the train, its snaking interior. People look into the camera.

While watching the film, I feel this is everything I want art to be. Perhaps the film resonates because all summer I have felt pain at my family's absence, their seeming lack of interest, my longing for my mother to still be alive. The elegiac feel of it. That Akerman and her mother are both dead. That this industrial New York is no more. The historical poignancy of the final shot of the receding skyline, while pulling out on the Staten Island Ferry, the twin towers in the distance.

Last night it took hours to get home from teaching uptown—all the stairs everywhere. Lately, I dream of stairs. How slow I must be. How I must consider movement. Yesterday I had the momentary fantasy that I could take off my stomach for the day and walk around. How I long for that lightness. My whole body is constantly sore and tender. All night I shift from side to side groaning—my hips, my pelvis.

Weeping again from the responses in my inbox from my department chairs. I get contractions when I weep. Yes, I can cancel class, but I must make it up, or get a substitute, for which they either have no budget or can pay very little, which makes it almost impossible to try to get a substitute. I'm being difficult, that's the undercurrent of the responses. My department head at the university writes to me that with luck everything will go without complications—she went to a party the week she gave birth, she writes. Sat the baby on the couch. Maybe it'll be the same for me. It's unbelievable. I forward all these emails to Suzanne, who shares my rage, which is my grief, our adjuncting lives, how little power we have. How am I supposed to make class up when I give birth weeks before the semester ends? I will be raw and bleeding. And, more than that, my midwives warn me that it will hurt my ability to heal, to nurse, if I go back to teaching a week after I give birth. Something won't feel right, one of them says to me. Suzanne suggests that I take time off, the next semester, for nursing and bonding. But I have to work! I cannot afford not to teach. And there's nowhere for us to move to, now. I need to finish *Drifts* to receive the rest of the advance, to pay for John's two months of unpaid paternity leave, to pay for the hospital bill, the midwives, to pay for everything. I want to just quit—everything—then what? I already cannot afford childcare, which I desire, to continue writing. This pregnancy exacerbates everything.

You need a bitchy pregnant friend, Sofia writes to me, in sympathy. Marie and I text each other our complaints. Our exhaustion and melancholy. How weird and volatile we are feeling. The underside of the now incessant congratulations. Sometimes we will text each other for an hour, sentences punctuated by a series of emojis: the strong arm, the heart, the weeping face. But what can Marie, who has a nanny and a night nurse on call, really understand about my adjunct woes?

Have been trying lately to practice extreme forbearance.
Now the subtle torture of an almost imperceptible rash of
tiny raised bumps on my hands and feet. John smooths
cortisone cream on my hands and feet—he rubs oil on my
pubic mound as it's getting too difficult to reach. I wash
with pine-tar soap. At night lukewarm oatmeal baths. I
sat on ice this morning—itchiness in vagina, sore pelvic
area. She's now head-down, says our midwife. Woke up
from non-nap, itchy, restless. Nervous exhaustion. In-
flamed, generally. Impossible to think or write.

I've been snapping the same selfies in front of our closet
mirror, next to the laundry hamper. The same print of
the royal blue rhomboid behind me. I put them up online. Yesterday was the first time I felt like myself in a
while—all black, black socks (because of the rash) and
Birkenstock clogs, the only shoes I can stuff my swollen
feet into, my lightweight frock coat, the long jersey
dress that has stretched to fit me. Harried, sunglasses
on head, black rubbery Swatch watch on my wrist.

On a rush-hour train people go out of their way now not to see me. The dude who refused to look up from his paperback *Bonfire of the Vanities* to see the heavily pregnant woman swaying irritated above him. I have to announce myself to prevent people (men) from shoving me or pushing into me on the train. Everyone feels they're more rushed, more exhausted, than everyone else. I feel the baby responding to a busker on the trumpet behind me, playing along to recorded elevator music. Now he's playing "New York, New York" as we ascend on the bridge. I am glad my bad attitude has returned. I feel more myself.

I fear the baby will be born on the day of the election.

I've had to be incredibly resilient, this mutely moving body, to get through rush hours and train transfers and hours of student meetings. I don't recognize myself in this uncomfortable and unbearable body. How she spins inside of me. What will become of me? I don't know. This cleaving, this rupture.

I fell asleep in the bathtub, then again on the toilet last night.

I wake up and read all the news about the election. How I have hated men in public throughout this pregnancy, how I play chicken with beer-necked men at Grand Central, who barrel through, insisting that everyone get out of their way—my witchy refusal to allow these men to push in front of me, I write to Sofia.

The strange almost-erotics of alienation that you mention, she writes to me. Perhaps, she writes, one loves one's alienation, painful as it is, as a kind of survival strategy, a way of loving the self. Or maybe it's not a strategy, one just gets used to it, the alienation, until it becomes like the scent of one's own skin.

There's so much dread about being an artist and a writer once you've become a mother, I write to Sofia. I wonder how much I've internalized it. My thinking and writing felt more sensitive and intense than ever, before the pregnancy, and pregnancy has only magnified this. Despite the slowness and heaviness, I feel a real potency and lucidity. I think I'm glad this has happened. This de-creation. This complete overwriting of the self.

In 1908, René Maria moves into the Hôtel Biron, a former convent of Sacré-Cœur, a gray mansion with a field
of weeds converted into artists' studios. He will occupy
this space, with its soaring ceilings and three bay windows, on and off over the next couple of years, in another attempt to work on the novel. Because he cannot
afford any furniture, the sculptor, with whom he has re-
connected, gifts him a large oak table. He looks out over
an abandoned garden. Rabbits leap across the trellis as
across an ancient tapestry, he writes Rodin, who likes it
so much when he visits it that he rents out an entire floor
for his city studio; later, the entire building becomes
the museum to the sculptor's work. There is a portrait
photograph of Rilke sitting at this table in 1908, looking pensively into the distance. He is most likely not at
work on the novel, which exists entirely in loose forms,
mostly letters and notebooks. But at the New Year he
promises to commit himself to the novel—no more poetry collections, no more receiving visitors or taking
vacations until it is finished that summer. His publisher
has agreed to give him a monthly salary if he writes the
novel by that deadline. However, three women visit him
in Paris that year: his wife, his mentor, and a new love
interest. In two haunted nights he writes a requiem to

Paula, who died weeks after giving birth—an embolism, so sudden that her last word was *Schade!* (A pity!) He travels for half the year. But by winter of 1909 he must truly confront the novel. Except for two vacations, he spends the rest of the year in Paris at the hotel, writing and rewriting. He has promised to remain cloistered inside the hotel, locking himself in his drafty room, taking meals through a little sliding window. To write the novel, he must cease to exist. It was in these rooms that he rewrote these scenes of childhood. He writes, in a letter, that he is beginning to feel the space around him become vast. It is here, in a beloved city, that he writes about memories of the same city, which he then despised. It is here, after he was famous, that he hid out and pretended to be a nobody, the twenty-eight-year-old barely published poet, writing alone in his room. For a city is not linear. How fiction works in repetition until it takes a final form. How many iterations and foldings of time a novel can take. And what is a novel but an immense solitude? He tells his publisher in May that he cannot finish by August as planned. By the fall of 1909, sick, fluish, exhausted, he spends three weeks recovering at the Black Forest spa. Still sick, he returns to Paris in October to wrestle again with this work. Most of the text exists only in a mass of small notebooks, scattered parts of old manuscripts, scraps of paper, letters and ripped-out diary pages, disconnected scenes and episodes. Nothing like a first draft. He fails to assemble a coherent manuscript. He can't get a sense of the whole. Finally, his publisher invites him to stay at his mansion outside of Leipzig. He will give him rooms, away from their two little girls. He arrives with a trunk filled with these tiny notebooks and notes. For two weeks, in a small quiet room in a tower, he dictates the novel to a typist. By the beginning of 1910, he has finished the book. Once it is published, Rilke surrenders to a total crisis of the self, exhausted from the experience, feeling perhaps that he has spent himself, that he will never write again. More than a decade of restless wanderings follow, an entirely itinerant existence. In 1914 alone he travels to Paris, Berlin, Munich, Zurich, Paris, Duino, Venice, Milan, Paris, Leipzig, Munich, Eschershausen, Munich, Frankfurt, Würzburg, and Berlin again.

Teary talks with John about our future. I think of giving in to his constant desire to quit everything and buy a cheap farmhouse upstate. So you could still be a thinking person, he says. But I would still have to commute hours to teach, more than I already do. And I keep envisioning myself alone in a Walmart with the baby in the grocery cart, stuck in some rural area, more isolated than ever. The Rilkes were miserable in their farmhouse, I keep reminding John. They worried about money constantly. That would be us. We don't have enough money to stay here, or to leave, we are drained, depleted, the alienation of adjunct labor, the fear of actual labor. I sit here with my hard shell of a body and cannot be soothed.

Sofia just taught Gabriel García Márquez's story "A Very Old Man with Enormous Wings." Her students complained that it was boring and had no point. Of course, Sofia writes, this made her want to champion strange, boring stories with no point. I read the story. A newborn sick baby. A very old angel stuck in the mud, then kept in a cage like an animal. I had just described to John, as we held each other, that I felt like a sore egg or a grotesque angel, some new hard-shell form I couldn't recognize. As I write this, the baby keeps kicking my ribs.

This morning, wearing a long-sleeved black-and-white-striped tee with my belly hanging out, I see the old woman. She asks us if it's Monday. I smilingly tell her it is. She jokes, I have to ask my cat to check the calendar.

For my notebook seminar, we read some of Virginia Woolf's journals. In one entry, Woolf writes of having only fifteen minutes that day to write in her notebook. I write this fact to Sofia, overwhelmed by the semester. I wish I had written of the weekend, its fullness, softness, its privacy, how liminal this waiting period, there still is beauty in all of this.

Constant communication all week from the Italian clown
upstairs. Playing his new set of drums all day Sunday, when
we needed space and silence to work on the layout for the
mother book. On Tuesday, a belligerent email asking what
times during the day he can practice drums. (Never!) Then,
yesterday, a shipment of music equipment—to be delivered,
he specifies in a note, to my unit, as I will be home to sign for
it, which I refuse. Worst of all, his pacing upstairs. Just the
two of us during the day. I feel cornered.

The cat might be back. John takes a photograph of her on
the porch. He keeps on seeing her. She's looking for us!
I exclaim.

A gloomy, rainy, humid Saturday. In bed all afternoon,
writing emails instead of notes in my journal. John came
home at noon from tennis at the park and laid around on
the bed with us, Genet basking in his body, licking his
sweat all over him. How the dog luxuriates in John's body
when he's home, how we both do—and how we luxuriate
in the dog, scratching, cuddling, rubbing. I worry over
him getting enough affection. Give him a kiss too! I tell
John in the morning.

The eternal mandatory hospital class. There is a Danish woman who shares my due date, yet she is so tall and slim, like we are not the same species. The doula leading the class, an Orthodox Jewish woman, says that we moms shouldn't cook or clean for four weeks, when we're not nursing we should lie around and watch Bravo for a month. When she says this word—moms—I flinch. It's the first time I've thought of that term, applied to myself by a stranger. Also I appreciate thinking about the time the postpartum body needs to heal, but this is not always allowed under capitalism, I must return to teaching. And also, my soul would die watching only Bravo for a month, I need to watch trash and then also read something abstruse and email Sofia about it. Maggie Nelson writing of how the thinking pregnant woman is seen as an anomaly, an extension of the anomaly of the thinking woman, and this feels true. How I've never felt more overdetermined by my body, as a woman, than when I've been pregnant. How cute and normative pregnant people are seen to be. And yet, conversely, how totally goth pregnancy actually is. Sofia asks me if we've bought the stroller yet. I'm refusing to think about any of it. My ambivalences toward parenthood manifested by the prospect of the mammoth stroller—to have to navigate such a thing here.

Thursday night on Metro-North heading home experiencing unbearable intestinal distress—I felt sure I would
shit myself on the train, in the dark tunnel, sitting next to
a businessman on his tablet—I ran to the toilet at Grand
Central, holed up in there, exploded my insides while
tearfully texting John. Contractions afterward from the
spastic diarrhea.

Mid-October. The surprise of summer weather today. Genet and I are out on what will likely be one of our last porch times of the season. I feel melancholy lately, luxuriating in the dog. Everyone tells me I will feel differently for Genet once the baby comes, and while I don't want to believe that, I mourn my time with him, our last solitude together. Will I even be able to sit on the porch, just the two of us, afterward? I feel I might be undergoing an immense hibernation, even from myself. He bathes in the sun and watches me, his amber eyes glowing. I read somewhere that your animal begins to stick close to you as labor approaches. Last night he laid himself across my back and nestled his chin into the small of my back as I slept. My body so large and heavy and slow yet needing pleasure—my animal, a hot shower, an orgasm. The other night John smoothed lotion all over my dry body and that too—a pleasure. But so often I feel chaotic, grotesque. I am stared at wherever I go. I am laboring more when walking. Even sitting at home, watching the dog sunbathe, drinking a glass of water—remembering the heat of last fall, how apocalyptic it felt—the return of the Halloween decorations—there is a pleasure and beauty to this, all of it both cyclical and fleeting. How changed my body is. The sky could not be more blue and the leaves more glowing and still green today.

Genet is up, chasing a fly. I coo to him in the voice I use to calm him. We stare at each other. I am supposed to give over to an animal state—that's what the books say, the ones I threw away.

We are told that the dog spends so much time in the
front room because he is on the lookout. A trainer
charges us $150 to tell us that. The same trainer who
can't get Genet to stop humping her and tells us to give
him cheese treats, which gives him severe gas. I am not
managing to do much in the office, except take photos
of myself on the computer in my ripped tank top at my
desk, blank notebook page in front of me, and measure
that photo against the portrait Paula Modersohn-Becker
painted of herself gently pregnant, although she wasn't
yet, at the moment in Paris when she completed the
painting, on the cusp of her potential. So I go into the
room and sit in the chair, watch Genet sleeping with his
chin propped up on the arm of the couch, smacking his
lips, still opening his eyes to survey the garbage truck to
make sure there are no intruders. It is 9:30 a.m. We've
been up several hours. Stress dream last night: I was
falling, falling, through a department store. Like Jimmy
Stewart in *Vertigo*.

A young man comes up to me on the day train as I'm
heading uptown to the midwives' for a pelvic exam, then
the Agnes Martin show at the Guggenheim, where I will
have to sit down or take a break after every circle around
the spiraled floor. He introduces himself, tells me he is a
fan. He is attractive. I am embarrassed by this fact, and
that I am so hugely pregnant. I awkwardly give him my
hand. My fingers so swollen I can no longer wear my
rings. I'll probably never see you again, he says, I needed
to say hello. He gets off at the next stop. My face is red.
A couple people were watching the interaction, and are
looking at me curiously, as if wondering if I am someone.
Their gaze goes quickly back to wherever they'd been
looking before. How odd it felt that I can still be recog-
nized. It's the notebook, I think, that gave me away.

There is a new cat, a large gray kitten, who hides behind the chair on the front porch, waiting for my striped cat to finish eating. The two cats coexist uneasily with each other. The little striped cat now comes twice a day to be fed. The gray kitten seems friendly, not feral. Perhaps abandoned. We study both of them—do they seem more lumpy, could they be pregnant or have worms? I scrolled through lost-cat forums yesterday, thought of putting up a flyer for the gray cat. I feel responsible for them. I can't touch them because of my allergies. I won't name them. I feel I can't give them the shelter they need. I almost don't want to see them sometimes, so that I won't have to worry. Although, on the days I don't see them, I still worry over them. I just looked out the window—it's pouring out—and sure enough the gray cat is finishing the food in the shelter of the porch. I watch her go over to the corner behind the chair, where Genet hangs out on sunny days. At least she can be dry there. I pick the dog up from his surveillance perch and make him come to the couch with me. He scrambles up to the top of the couch, behind my shoulders, chin on my head. We watch the rain.

How time is slowing and quickening at once. It is 5:30 a.m. The day before Halloween. I feel her kinetic force inside me. Every night lately it seems I have been up at 4 a.m. I can hear the buffoon stirring upstairs, having just come home—hyperaware that he hears me stirring, my movements, the bed constantly creaking under my weight. Lately I have not been able to bear it—I wake John up, ask him to touch my body, to hold my hand, to put his hands on me. The night before last I had lain down, completely naked, on top of all the covers. In bed, on my phone, I googled "can you feel your cervix efface?" Yesterday I was thirty-eight weeks. We took the train downtown. Men asking for change hollered at John *Good job* for impregnating me, asking if I was having twins or triplets. Always men on the street, the ones who used to tell me to smile, who now tell me how huge I am—some reverse form of catcalling. Everyone tells me how big I am. I've never seen a pregnant belly so large, a woman at the hair salon says to me. Why do you think you need to tell me that? I reply to her. It feels good to be snotty. You're huge! Marie exclaims when she sees me.

We go to the Pipilotti Rist show. What pure happiness
being there. Walking through her *Pixel Forest*, the beauty
and ecstasy of the saturated colors in her hanging light
installation. How buoyant, to lie there in public on a bed,
gazing at the ceiling screens, underneath a rotting leaf
drifting by in the water, a lily pad. A naked body swimming. A close-up of a nipple. I feel lighter, being there.

John is again talking of leaving, of us drifting somewhere
else. I don't want to move. I just want more time. I want
him home, raising the baby with me, in some utopian and
impossible arrangement I can't imagine. Where we both
can think and write and make things. I read that, when
Pipilotti Rist found out she was pregnant, she and her
partner went to raise their child on a beach somewhere.
If only we had resources to do that. But I also worry what
will happen to the gray stray with green eyes whom we
feed twice a day, and who seems to have adopted us. And
to my little striped cat of course.

It is November now. Every night some sort of possible alarm. A contraction? Is this it? We watch the baby's feet stick out, squirm across the surface of my abdomen. Staying up to watch the end of *The Matrix* on TV. (That scene where Neo rushes into the agent's body, that's what I feel like, without the explosion of white light.)

I keep trying to capture the gray cat on the porch, to take her to the vet, who has agreed to foster her. She keeps scrambling to the top of the neighbor's fence, where I can't reach her.

A bizarre occurrence on the 1 train yesterday. I sit in the corner seating, my bag on my lap. A man comes in, takes up two entire seats next to me, jostles me. I hold my arm firm, not allowing him to encroach on my space, trying to reclaim my seat. He then elbows me hard in the side. "You hit me, I hit you back," he shouts at me. He repeats it, more calmly, happy with himself. A woman makes sympathetic eye contact but says nothing. I sit frozen next to the man the rest of the ride, not knowing what to do, whether to get up, fearing an encounter. His violence, his aggression, how pleased with himself. The tumor of this election.

The baby is now five days overdue. The election. I am
in bed with Genet, eating a turkey sandwich. John went
to work, to try to store up as much of his unpaid leave
as possible. Weeping this morning. How this waiting is
wearing on me. I have been all hard, sore, contracting
body for a week—for weeks. I am living in some other
time. But outside of time as well. Yet I feel—also—the
panic, horror, and dread. Like everything has turned
upside down. A doubled sense of unreality. This hazy
nightmare state. I wake up sweating.

Today, needing to feel myself again, I attempt a few pages
of *Rings of Saturn*. To trace the layered way time works
in the novel—the narrator recollecting his walking tour
from the year before, while recovering from surgery in
the hospital. He looks at the grid of a window in his room
and thinks about Gregor Samsa remembering when he
found pleasure looking out the window when in human
form. That's how I feel now. My hard belly sticking out.

The week before I am to give birth, I get a letter from Sofia, still writing to me about literature, which is a relief to me, although I don't respond. She sends me a quote from Barthes's *The Neutral*—Kafka comparing himself to a "kavka," a jackdaw, whose wings have atrophied. "I hop about bewildered among my fellow men. They regard me with deep suspicion. And indeed I am a dangerous bird, a thief, a jackdaw. But that is only an illusion. In fact, I lack all feeling for shining objects. For that reason I do not even have glossy black plumage. I am gray, like ash. A jackdaw who longs to disappear between the stones."

Relatives, friends email me wanting updates. Students wanting letters of recommendation. I don't respond to anyone's messages. It all feels in the distance. What do I see. Yellow leaves. A return, I remember, to last fall. I escape with John and the dog on a brisk walk to attempt to push through these contractions. The almost sublime palette of fall colors. I notice the trees again. Her head settles into my pelvis.

I am in a wordless state, I write to Suzanne after I don't respond to a cluster of her texts, annoyed and abjected, her ex having just won a major literary award.

Genet now asleep on the dark gray blanket at the foot of the bed. I read today that dogs can smell time.

I have had to write my editor that I cannot turn in *Drifts* before the baby comes, as I had hoped. I beg an extension until February. Perhaps when John is home, perhaps then I can work. . . .

December 7

I have only written down the date, and John and Genet have come into the bedroom. The baby is asleep on my lap. She is a week and a half old. I can address her little presence in front of me. As I was stoned and woozy on the pain days, I wrote in my mind delirious odes to her sweaty dark hair curling against her neck in a rattail, her dark eyes, mischievous and thoughtful, her chubby cheeks, the scarlet blotches that appear all over her tiny body, the dark fur on the delicate rolls of her back. She stirs and wiggles and belches and farts and groans on my lap. This babbling and cooing creature. She scratches at my breasts, leaving red marks. The pull of nursing, lying there in our diapers, bellies pressed against each other, feeling some electricity run through my body. She is wild—I didn't realize that. How elegant and force-ful the acrobatics of her body twisting and contorting, kicking me—like she did all those months inside me, with such insistency. Right now my major affect is only intense exhaustion from night feedings. I am grateful for that. She pecks at my chest and I must stop writing. She has her witching hour in the early evening—then she is bright red, inconsolable. We rock her and sing her songs. We are a household of shit, even more than before. My unbearable constipation and hemorrhoids, her explosions, the dog's. We fart and shit and walk around barely clothed.

I finally left the house today, after at least a week indoors. The baby cried in her over-huge bear suit. We all walked briskly around the block.

That we will remember these days as beautiful in their urgency, I just realized. When did Rilke grow tired of it?

I am beginning to repair. Now I feel only soreness, pain from the stitches, and exhaustion. Yet I don't know how to acknowledge the raw sensation of my wound—the last month of prodromal labor, the trauma and medical intervention of the labor and delivery—how vulnerable and naked I have felt.

How time worked at the end. How I would labor at night, and be up in the day. Every date began to take on a ghostly meaning. How I couldn't read or write anything, but John read out loud Simone Weil's *Gravity and Grace* to me on the train, in the days before being induced at the hospital, feeling my contractions as the train bounced. Simone Weil attempting to philosophize and endure her own personal suffering, her raging headaches, while floating away from the self into grace. "Grace is the law of the descending movement."

And then afterward. Alone in the hospital bed, in the middle of the night, the baby asleep. I felt so sure in that pain and abjection that I wouldn't be able to write about Rilke anymore. That I wouldn't be able to write of the self I had been before—and then who even was this shattered being?

But here I am still, in my bedroom, balancing my notebook on my pulsating, red-faced, sleeping baby, propped
up on a pillow. Staring at the window. Meditating on the
pillows on the bed, Genet on another pillow next to me,
on alert, my mind wandering to the sketches of pillows
Dürer made on the verso of a self-portrait, alongside a
disembodied drawing hand poised and floating over yet
another pillow. These experiments in form.

The first moment I wrote in my notebook again, I wrote
of that fleeting feeling in the morning, of possibility.
That's what I want *Drifts* to be, my desire and longing
for it.

And how long did it take to make my way back into my
office afterward, to sit at my desk and stare at the oversize
book, open up there for more than two years now, the
facing images I'm still staring at in this moment? Dürer's
Melencolia I—how I've thought of her these years. This
room I now share with the changing table and bureau and
crib and books and toys. When did I realize that it is her
baby in *Melencolia I*—her baby, their mess, the day.

Still, what the beautiful is, I know not, although, it adheres to many things. . . .

ACKNOWLEDGMENTS

This book would not exist without my principal correspondent Sofia Samatar, an important reader and collaborator. To Danielle Dutton, Bhanu Kapil, Suzanne Scanlon, T Clutch Fleischmann, and Amina Cain, who have represented the possibilities of literary community for me. Love as well to all my other correspondents.

This book also wouldn't be possible if it weren't for Cal Morgan, whose belief in this work has helped bring it to its final form. Thank you to everyone at Riverhead. To Philomene Cohen, for her assistance. And to Sofia Groopman, for being an early champion, and as always Mel Flashman.

This project is indebted to the collaboration and engagement of my partner, John Vincler—who was invaluable in helping conceptualize the visual aspects of the book, particularly the collages, and who is one of the most brilliant writers and thinkers about art that I know.

To my daughter, Leo. For making me think so constantly about beauty and joy.

This book, as I reread it, seems ultimately dedicated to my little zen master Genet, to his love and friendship, what he's taught me about how to live. Perhaps he'll lick the photo of me, if it appears, if the book is left out on the porch, in the sun.